THE SCREWDRIVER KILLER

A chilling crime thriller with a stunning final twist

EMMY ELLIS

DI Bethany Smith Book 3

Originally published as *Red is the Colour*

JOFFE BOOKS

Revised edition 2023
Joffe Books, London
www.joffebooks.com

First published in Great Britain in 2019
as *Red is the Colour*

This paperback edition was first published
in Great Britain in 2023

Cover art by Dee Dee Book Covers

ISBN: 978-1-83526-114-9

PROLOGUE

Hate. It festered in you.
Always there. Burning.

The dried pieces of flesh looked strange on the dessert spoon, all crinkled like that. They reminded him of pomegranate seeds or those bacon bits some restaurants threw on a salad. Maybe he ought to mix them with other food to give it the appearance of being something else entirely. Edible. He'd feed it to the bastards who'd upset him and smile, knowing what they were really eating. The small nodules had been stored in a plastic tub since Mother had died, the meat of her backside, just a slice off one cheek.

No need to be greedy, was there.

He took some jam from the fridge and blended the two things together in a bowl.

That should do nicely.

His phone rang. A shufti at the screen showed the name he'd been hoping for — she'd taken far too long to respond. Selondra. Such a bitch.

"There's no chemistry, Harry," she'd said.

He hadn't understood what she'd meant. Still didn't. What did chemistry have to do with anything? You poked your willy in her hole, and that was the end of that, wasn't it? She'd wanted him to do things he wasn't comfortable with, like touching her nipples. Who *did* that? Those were for babies to drink milk from.

Harry swiped to answer the call. "Hi, so wonderful to hear from you." *At last.*

"What do you want?" she said. "There have been several calls from you today, and you clearly haven't got the message that if I don't answer, it means I don't want to know. I rather thought I'd made that clear the last time we spoke."

The hairs on the back of his neck stood up at that. Who did she think she was, the cheeky strumpet? "I'm royalty. You shouldn't speak to me like that."

She laughed as though he wasn't right in the head. "Oh, for fuck's sake. Extremely diluted royalty."

"Still royalty."

"What, a super-distant bloody cousin of some earl or other? So distant that you don't even figure? Sorry, but I won't fall for that line again."

"Let me make it up to you," he said, going for pleading. That was supposed to work with the ladies. Apparently, they usually felt sorry for you and gave in if you begged hard enough. That hadn't happened with Mother, though.

"By doing what?" Selondra asked.

He imagined her tapping her foot on the floor and folding her bottom lip over her teeth. An annoying habit. One that had him wanting to punch her nose until it disappeared into her face. "I'll cook you dinner."

She'd liked his food in the past.

"Hmm. Maybe." She sighed. "What's for pudding?"

Was she being rude? Asking about dessert and meaning a different kind?

Innuendo, that was what it was called, so one of his new books said.

She went on, "You know I don't like missionary pudding."

A jibe. She was good at those.

"I want to try a lovely brulée with a strawberry preserve." He gritted his teeth to stop himself from laughing, but it bubbled up, pressing to come out. "There will be yummy pieces in it. What do you think?"

"Bloody hell! Okay. When?"

"Tonight?"

"Short notice, Harry."

"I'll make it worth your while." *You have to agree. Don't make me come out there and find you. You must be here. Tonight.*

Another sigh. "Fine. Eight o'clock?"

"That's brilliant. Wear your black dress. The one with the sequins all over it." If she turned up in that, he'd have no problem getting angry when he needed to. That dress had been the beginning of the end for her.

"Whatever. Catch you later. Toodle-oo." She hung up on him.

He put his phone on the worktop, his eyes fuzzing over until the screen went dark, obliterating the image of the earl's family crest. He clamped his jaw at her saying 'Toodle-oo', like she was royalty herself instead of a rich hanger-on who just wanted to marry into more money.

She wouldn't be marrying anyone.

Not unless you could do that in Heaven.

CHAPTER ONE

"What am I supposed to be seeing here?" Bethany asked, grumpy at being put on the spot. She was cold — autumn was a frozen bitch this year — and hadn't had much sleep because some neighbour's cat had howled to be let in for what had seemed like half the bloody night.

She scrutinised the papers on her office desk.

Isabelle, the lead SOCO, frowned. "Can't you see it? Look harder."

Bethany did. The copies of the map and letter appeared the same as when she'd opened the envelope and seen the originals. They'd arrived the other day at the station by post. The map had been drawn by hand, a crude rendering, like a kid had done it. Multiple trees in a cluster had two lines for trunks and clouds on top for leaves. A road, winding, with dashes down the middle to show what it was. A hill with a dot beside it. A row of five large flowers, much bigger than the trees.

"I'm not seeing anything." Bethany was at a loss. "The dot is significant, where the body supposedly is, but this map gives us sod all. The site could be anywhere. The flowers are probably the killer's way of saying they're sorry — that they represent a grave."

"But what if we've been seeing this wrong? What if they're not flowers?" Isabelle poked a finger at them. "When people draw them, the petals are usually round, with six or more present. This has three, and they're spiky."

"I just took it to be daisies where some had been picked off. You know: he loves me, he loves me not. They even have the circle in the middle and stems."

"Yes, the shape of the petals is similar to a daisy, but see how spaced out they are? What does it seem like to you?"

"Someone can't draw, that's what it seems like." Bethany was getting arsey. She preferred to just be told straight, not go around the houses. Playing guessing games wasted time and got her goat.

"What about wind turbines?" Isabelle suggested.

Bethany's heart fluttered. "Shit . . . Where are—?"

"Five miles away — I found that out before I came here and know exactly where this is anyway because I go there. Shadwell Hill." She took another, proper map out of the file on the desk and put the other one on top. "Here is where the turbines are on the real map. There's the hill, the road, the trees. At a guess, the turbines are about half a mile away from the hill on the right. The dot is in a direct line from the closest turbine."

"So I gather you didn't get any prints off the originals," Bethany said, "or anything significant about the paper used?"

"No." Isabelle shook her head. "Common A4 paper bought for home printers. The person must have worn gloves. Bic ballpoint pen, something along those lines. Nothing we can use."

Bethany stopped herself from swearing, not that Isabelle would mind if she did.

She studied the letter again.

Dear Police,

I did a vile thing. There's a body at the dot. Have fun working out where that is.

Watch your step when you get there.

From,

Me

"Is that area boggy or something?" Bethany asked. "I've never been out that way."

"It's a nice place to walk the dog. Pretty forest, and that hill is big. Craggy, like a mountain. Some people climb it. But no, it's not boggy there. Even in winter it's okay to visit."

"It's been bugging me since I first read it, what they mean by 'watch your step'."

"Animal traps, maybe?"

"Surely someone or their pet would have been caught in one by now if it's a place people take dogs."

"Hmm. Either way, we're going to have to go out there."

"Is it accessible by car? What I mean by that is, can we get pretty close to the dot?"

"Yes, the road goes past the hill. There's flat land in one section, grass, a picnic area, so we could drive over it. Going by the drawn map, though, we'd have to go through forest a short way to get to the dot."

"Okay. Let's get going."

It didn't take long, and they were on their way, Isabelle in the SOCO van, Bethany and Mike following. Presley, the ME, tagged along behind them in his beloved blood-red car. They parked as close to the forest area as they could and all got out, then togged up in protective clothing, receiving a freaked-out glance from a woman with a poodle carrying a stumpy stick in its mouth. Bethany asked her if she'd seen anything out of the ordinary going on here lately, but the lady shook her head.

They trooped through the forest, following the coordinates someone from Isabelle's team had worked out, and came to within a hundred metres or so from the foot of the hill, trees still around them.

"It's just a case of scouting this area," Isabelle said.

"Be careful where you're walking," Bethany reminded them all. "We've had a warning about watching our step, whatever that means."

Everyone else separated, but Bethany and Mike remained where they were.

"I want to get a good recce before we go anywhere," she told him.

"I agree." Mike nodded. "I'd rather get my bearings first."

Weak sunlight made a valiant attempt at sneaking in through the autumn-kissed branches, which were heavy with leaves of gold, red, and green on the late turn. Many coated the ground, a layer disturbed by walkers and pets who'd been there since the killer had deposited the body — if one had even been dumped. This could all be an elaborate hoax. Since the map and note had arrived, they'd had nothing to go on until today, so numerous clues would have been compromised in the meantime.

A shout — or more like a male scream — came from up ahead, and Bethany faced Mike for a second, then they were off, heading in that direction. A circle of SOCOs stood to the left, and Bethany approached, Mike close behind. She nudged between two people and stared.

A hole.

"What's going on?" Bethany asked.

"Ted fell through," Isabelle said. "The ground just appeared normal, then he was gone."

Watch your step.

Leaves must have blanketed it, and long branches had been revealed, criss-crossed over the two-metre-wide hole, a large gap at the edge where Ted had stepped onto the disguised forest floor and gone through.

"Get back to the van and bring rope," Isabelle told a female officer. "Also bring the large torch." She knelt beside the hole. "Won't be long, Ted."

Bethany moved forward and went down on her haunches to peer over. Ted gawped up at her, thankfully on his feet, leaves and forest debris on his shoulders. He was about five metres down. Someone had dug this — and would have needed quite some time to do it. Saying that, the sides were a bit too smooth for it to have been done over several nights with a shovel. Seemed a machine of some sort had been used to slice down.

"You okay?" she asked Ted.

"Yep, shaken up more than anything."

The SOCO came back from the van, and Isabelle tied the end of the rope around the torch handle and lowered it to Ted.

"Have a nose around down there, will you?" she said.

Ted switched the torch on and flashed the beam about. "Um, there's food wrappers here — energy bars — and a flask."

What? Had someone been kept in there? Was that person the dead body they'd yet to find?

Bethany stood and turned to Mike. "We need to get cracking."

While a couple of SOCOs held the rope, one behind the other, and Ted climbed up, the rest, plus Bethany and Mike, walked carefully, a small step at a time in case there were more holes. They moved closer to the foot of the hill, where the trees thinned out to nothing, revealing the hillside.

Another shout, to the left again. "Mound!"

Fuck.

Bethany grabbed a long stick and poked the ground ahead as they went that way. "Can one of you do what I'm doing and scour the whole area, please?" she called. "We don't need anyone falling down another sodding hole."

Someone waved at her in acknowledgement, and she pressed on, prodding the forest floor, nervous in case the end of the stick disappeared beneath the leaves and she swiftly followed into a hole. Safely at the mound, where a huddle of SOCOs gathered, Bethany scoped it out. The earth hadn't been covered over with leaves. Instead, it was out on full display, bobbles of it, an oblong mountain of Maltesers. A body-sized mountain.

"Shit." Bethany sighed. She'd hoped the letter and map had been some kids messing about for a joke. No such pissing luck. "All right, over to you and yours, Isabelle. Can you message me when you get to the body?"

Isabelle nodded.

While the photographer got on with his job, Bethany and Mike moved away — it'd be a long wait while the SOCOs removed the soil, bagged it, and unearthed the body. They had somewhere they needed to be, but first, she had to get her head screwed on straight.

"Okay, let's go through what we already know," she said to Mike. "The letter arrived on Friday, sent within Shadwell. First class, so popped in the mail the day before or late the night before that. We've got a map at the station with all the post offices and boxes on it."

Fran had used pins with coloured balls on the ends so they had a clear view of what was what, black for the offices, red for boxes. There were hundreds of boxes, what with it being a city.

"CCTV has been done — and that was a lot of work for us lot over three bloody days, wasn't it, *and* we lost our weekend by working," she said. "So that's brought us to now, Monday, and meanwhile, there's possibly a body rotting under that mound."

"Maybe it won't be too bad. The state of it, I mean," Mike said, scrubbing a wrist over his chin.

"Depends on when the person was killed."

Presley came over to join them, a lock of ginger hair peeking out from beneath his hood at his temple.

"Just the one we wanted to see," Bethany said. "You need to tuck your hair under, by the way. What do you think we've got here?"

Presley shrugged and did as she'd asked. "Soil slows decomposition, so we may get one that seems relatively fresh. Do you have a time scale?"

"If the body was buried around the time the person wrote the letter," — she explained what had been sent to the station — "then five days or so."

"Okay, we're possibly going to see a body that has begun purification on the inside with minimal visible signs of it on the outside apart from skin colour and whatnot. However, if bloat has occurred, and in some cases that can be so severe the skin splits from the internal pressure — gases, see — then we might have a more disgusting sight."

Bethany grimaced. "Lovely. Bloat. You've said before this is more likely when oxygen is present, so if the body was buried right away, we might not have to see any split skin. God. Well, this is going to take a while, so we may as well go and visit the place that runs the turbines, Mike, see if anyone saw anything weird going on."

Presley said, "I'm going to hang about. For once, I'm up to date at the lab." He waved and ambled off towards the mound.

* * *

Bethany and Mike reached the wind farm with the help of the satnav, and she shivered at the sheer size of the turbines, even though they were a fair way off in the distance. She hadn't appreciated just how big they were until now. The rotors reminded her of aeroplane propellers, and she laughed to herself for thinking they were flowers on that map.

She parked outside a massive warehouse-type building with a glass and steel overhang, and a sign on the front proclaiming it as Shadwell Wind Energy. They went inside, and a blonde woman sat behind a desk in a reception area. She smiled.

"Are you here for a tour?" She tilted her head, ponytail swishing.

Bethany produced her ID. "No. Can we see the manager?"

"Oh, of course." She jabbed a button on her phone. "Just got to wait for him to call back. He walks round with his mobile but sometimes doesn't hear it." Hers rang with an abrupt trill, and she picked it up. "The police are here to see you . . . Okay, will do." She came around to stand by them. "This way. Mr Vellord will speak to you now."

She took them through a doorway into what appeared to be a workshop full of machines that Bethany presumed monitored the electricity generated by the turbines. Workers stood or sat in front of them, and a forty-something man walked in their direction — grey suit trousers, white shirt. The receptionist left them to it. Bethany and Mike came to a stop beside a large computer, another man tapping at the keyboard, head bent.

Mr Vellord smiled. "Are you here about the theft of the boring apparatus?" He thrust out a hand.

They all shook.

With the pleasantries over and introductions made, Bethany asked, "Boring apparatus?" Her mind went a mile a minute with her thinking about the hole dug in the forest where Ted had fallen.

"Yes, some little scrote — uh, person — decided to break in and steal one of the borers. They're used to take out long, cylindrical sections of earth for us to put up our smaller turbines — and by smaller, I mean they're only four times the height of us. We decided to put them in so when the school kids come for tours, they can see them working better. Glad we have another borer, otherwise we'd be forking out in the near future as there are more turbines arriving soon. Mind you, I'm hoping our tool will be found by then because the job will get done faster with two."

"I see. When was it taken?" Bethany asked.

"Week before last."

The man at the computer coughed and frowned at them, then turned away to face his screen.

"Let's move," Mr Vellord said. "John likes peace when he's working."

They all shifted over to an area with some privacy.

"What day was it stolen?" Bethany smiled at Mr Vellord.

"Wednesday before last. The buggers got in overnight. Come the Thursday morning, I had a broken lock on our equipment section — from the outside — and a valuable tool was missing."

"Are all your employees aware of the tools you keep here?"

"Of course. Why do you ask?"

She thought it best to lower her voice in case John could still hear them. "We're actually here on another matter, but now you've mentioned the borer, I have a feeling I know what it was used for. What I wanted to know was whether you noticed any suspicious activity around here — out on the road maybe, a vehicle driving over the flat land by the hill."

"Can't say any of us would have. My employees are indoors for the most part, except for Yentis doing the daily turbine checks, and he'd have reported anything weird. I do the tours, and I haven't seen anything going on. What's happened then?"

"We're investigating a possible murder."

He paled. "Bloody hell. What's my borer got to do with it?" He blinked. "Oh. Are you saying it was used to make a hole to bury someone?"

"No." She wasn't going to tell him it might have created a hole big enough to keep someone captive in. "Can we see your other borer? It'll give us an idea of the size and how it may have been taken to the site in question."

"Come this way."

He led them to the back of the room, and they went through another door, down a hallway, and into a space where machinery stood.

"This is it here," he said, pointing to one that could possibly have been hefted into the back of a Transit. "You need a genny to fire it up, but ours is still here."

So whoever used the borer must have had their own generator — or brought this one back. If so, why not bring the borer, too?

"Do you have CCTV?" She cocked her head.

Mr Vellord nodded. "Already been asked the same by one of your lot when I reported the theft. We do, but it went on the fritz, and the company couldn't get out to fix it until yesterday. Something about folks being on holiday."

"That's a long time without that kind of security." *And convenient it broke in the first place.*

"It is. I was fair shitting myself, to be honest, so I got nighttime security in."

"I don't blame you. So did you question your staff?"

"The other officers did it. Called Eccles and Yates. Nice pair. No one knew anything about it, though."

Or if they did, they'd hidden it. "Okay. Well, thanks for your time. Can we talk to your employees now? Saves us coming back."

"Yep. They're all in the other room at the moment, so crack on. Lisa, the receptionist, well, you know where she is."

"Thanks," Bethany said.

Mr Vellord guided them back to the first room and strode off.

"Shall we split up?" she asked Mike.

He nodded, and they took half the room each. Bethany's lot hadn't seen or heard anything, and no one seemed suspicious, so she met up with Mike to question John, the last one.

"DI Bethany Smith and DS Mike Wilkins," she said to him. "Sorry to disturb, but we need to speak to you. What's your surname?"

He sighed and stopped typing, apparently annoyed at being interrupted, the crabby sod. "Cribbins. John Cribbins."

"Right." Bethany smiled in the hope it might thaw him a bit. "Where were you on the evening the borer was stolen?"

He reared his head back in shock. "Me? What the hell would I want a borer for?"

"I didn't ask what you wanted one for, I asked where you were."

He flushed and shifted on his stool. "At home or the pub. Where else would I be?"

"I don't know. You tell me."

"Well, I was at the pub. The Lamb Shank on the Shadwell Heights estate."

Bethany inwardly shuddered at the mention of that area. One of the main drug dealers lived there in a high-rise. The estate was full of wrongdoers and somewhere she didn't like to visit if she could help it. "Did you go with anyone?"

"Nope, but a few people saw me. Uncle Crack for one."

Why mention the dealer? All right, everyone on that estate knew who Uncle Crack was, but everyone also knew he would give you an alibi for a few quid.

"Are you into what he's selling then? Like a bit of weed, do you?" She raised her eyebrows.

"No, absolutely not." His answer came too quickly. "The landlord and barmaid saw me as well. Ask them if I was there."

"We will." Bethany smiled again, but not kindly this time. Something was well off here. "What did you do after you'd been to the Shank?"

"I went home. I don't make a habit of going out in the middle of the night, so I stayed in from eleven onwards."

"Who mentioned the middle of the night?"

"That's when the borer must have been taken."

"I don't see why. The CCTV wasn't working. It could have been taken at any point that evening or into the early hours."

"You're making me uneasy, accusing me of doing it."

Bethany turned to Mike. "Did you hear me accuse him?"

"Nope."

"Didn't think I did. Thank you for talking to us, Mr Cribbins."

She walked off, out into reception. After speaking to Lisa behind the desk and finding nothing of consequence, Bethany and Mike got in the car.

"He knows something, that John." Mike plugged his seat belt in.

"Too right. Reckon he has something to do with the borer going missing?"

"Yep."

"Same. Well, we'll leave him to sweat for a bit, then go back another day and question him again. If a borer was used to dig that hole, I want to know who stole it — and who they stole it for."

CHAPTER TWO

The air stank. Bethany held her breath and tried not to vomit. The body rested only a few inches down, and she was surprised some animal or other hadn't discovered the mound and had a good go at digging. Presley crouched beside it after assessing it visually for a time of death.

"A good few days," he said.

That much was obvious, but it was like he'd said earlier: it appeared relatively fresh apart from the grey-purple pallor and lividity on the underside — he'd lifted an arm to inspect for rigor, which had come and gone, but the skin there appeared as a massive bruise. No bloat splits. Always a relief.

"Unless the body tells me otherwise when I roll it," Presley said, "this woman was placed in this position, on her back, from the moment she'd died. There's no lividity on her sides or front."

Bethany gawked at the naked woman. Grey-white hair. Wrinkled skin. Around a size eight, all bones and not much flesh. Maybe seventy or so, give or take a few years either way. Someone's mother, sister, child. Someone loved. A nasty graze marred her cheek — well, graze was an understatement. It was more like a pile of red mash.

One of her eyes had been removed.

"Despite the state of that face, I recognise her," Mike said. "I'm a bit of a fan."

"A fan? And how the hell can you recognise *that* mess?"

"Going by the clear side, I'm sure she's Margaret Allthrop."

"And she is?"

"A woman far removed from the throne but royal nonetheless."

"Okay . . ."

With Fran and Leona already searching for elderly women who'd gone missing, Bethany would wait for one of them to call her so they could get a definite identity for the poor old girl.

Presley pushed the body onto its side. The skin was so dark, a palette of a stormy sky. Bethany forgot for a moment the lady was dead and winced at how sore it seemed, how the movement might have hurt.

"Fuck me, she's had some of her arse cheek cut off," Presley said.

"I beg your bloody pardon?" Bethany jolted at the news. Why would anyone want to cut *that* off? She leaned closer and wished she hadn't. A fresh waft of eau de dead sailed over her. "Christ, that smell is so awful. Any idea what was used to cut it?"

"Probably a knife. It's a nice and clean slice."

"Before or after death?"

"I'd say before. There's soil on the wound, but if you have a good gander, you can see where it's healed in some places and festered in others. Had a bit of an infection going on." He pointed to one section.

Bethany eyed Mike. "Reckon she was kept in that hole?"

He shrugged. "Ted's back in there now, collecting evidence. If one of her hairs or whatever is found, then that's your answer."

"Poor cow."

"She's meant to be in the Cotswolds," Mike said. "So it said on the online news anyway."

"How come I'm only just hearing about you following the society pages?"

"Thought you might laugh." He shrugged.

"Of course I wouldn't!"

Isabelle came over from where she'd been at the hole. "Oh. Unpleasant. Not something I want to see just before dinner, not that I'll be getting food anytime soon."

"What's unpleasant, the odour or the arse?" Presley grinned.

"Both. What's the bum business in aid of?" Isabelle pressed her hand to her nose.

"No bloody idea," Bethany said.

Presley examined the back of the head. "No contusions. No visible signs to indicate cause of death." He lowered her again. "Although her wrists have marks where she's been bound."

"We've found some impressions in the ground by the hole," Isabelle said. "Shifted the leaves and whatever away, and there's squares in the mud."

Bethany thought of the borer at the wind farm. "How many?"

"Four," Isabelle said.

"Could be the feet of the boring tool." She told her about the theft and the fact that the genny was still there.

"Then the genny wasn't placed on the ground with the borer," Isabelle said. "Might have been kept in a vehicle — there are tyre dips where maybe a van was parked for a while, but no tracks to show them driving in and out of here."

"Okay, I'm going with the assumption the borer is definitely something to do with this. So, we have a killer who either works at Shadwell Wind Energy or they know someone who does. The killer and or the machine thief could already own a generator. Why keep an old lady down a hole, though, where she could be discovered by a dog walker or jogger, or scream and be heard? And tell all — tell whoever found her the name or the description of the person who'd put her there? It doesn't make sense."

"These things usually don't." Isabelle waved. "I'm off over there." She wandered back to her team.

"I'm fucking baffled," Mike said.

Someone called out from behind them.

Bethany turned. "What's up?" She headed that way, Mike by her side, and came to a stop next to a SOCO on his hands and knees.

He'd moved a load of leaves to one side to reveal a sign used by road workers and the like. It had a metal frame with a yellow triangle and black font that read: DANGER. UNSTABLE AREA.

She said to Mike, "Used to keep people away while she was in the hole?"

"Seems likely. Because of who she is, maybe she was abducted for a ransom."

"But if she's sort of famous, why haven't we heard about her going missing?"

"Like I said, she's meant to be in the Cotswolds."

"There's rope here as well," the SOCO said, swiping some leaves away.

Yep, a coil of it.

"And what's that? The end of poles?" Bethany pointed to beside the rope.

The SOCO removed more leaves and branches. "Mud on the other ends of them. They could have been pushed into the ground and the rope was used as a cordon."

"Scheming bastard," Bethany said. "We have a killer who went the extra mile to make sure the lady wasn't discovered by randoms. I'm saying she was alive in the hole, otherwise, why the energy bars and flask?"

Mike sniffed. "Why keep her there at all if she was only going to be killed anyway?"

Bethany pondered that. "The killer might have a schedule and can't risk being away from home for long periods. They might have abducted her and needed somewhere to keep her. I don't know, but whatever went on, it still resulted in a death." Her phone bleeped. "Two seconds." She accessed her messages.

> Fran: TWO MISSING OLDER LADIES, BUT ONE WAS FOUND THIS MORNING. DEMENTIA, WANDERED OFF. YOU MIGHT HAVE THE OTHER. A MARGARET ALLTHROP, SIXTY-FIVE, THE GRANGE, THAT BIG HOUSE OUT ON WILLAMING ROAD.

>> Bethany: OKAY, THANKS. GET ON THAT AS IF SHE'S DEFINITELY OUR WOMAN — MIKE DID A VISUAL IDENTIFICATION. ANY RELATIVES?

> Fran: A SON. HARRY. LIVES AT THE GRANGE. HE REPORTED HER MISSING LAST THURSDAY.

>> Bethany: ANY IMAGES OF HER?

> Fran: YES. GOT A FEW FROM ONLINE. SHE'S IN THE LOCAL NEWS A LOT FOR CHARITY WORK ETC. I'LL SEND THEM IN A MO.

>> Bethany: THANKS, WE'LL GO TO THE GRANGE NOW.

"Got something?" Mike asked.

"Seems you're right and it's Margaret Allthrop."

"Christ." Mike widened his eyes.

"Great. With her being distant royalty, let's hope the queen doesn't get on our backs then." Bethany smiled. "Just joking." Her message alert went off again. "That'll be the images." She opened them, getting confirmation that the dead person was one and the same. She showed Mike.

"Yeah, that's her. Wonder why she got bumped off?"

"That's what we're here for, matey. Come on, we've got a son to see."

They said their goodbyes and drove to The Grange, a posh affair set back from the road in its own grounds, with a sweeping driveway and pruned poplars either side of it. Closer to the large stately home, hedges had been trimmed into the shapes of animals — a dragon, a cat, and some sort of mythical being resembling a fairy with horns. The home itself belonged in a pamphlet with the blaring headline on it saying: TOP PLACES TO VISIT IN SHADWELL. She'd passed it on numerous occasions but had never taken that much notice, what with it seeming so far away from the road. Now she was up close, it was clear it belonged to extremely rich people. Nobles, no matter how distant they were to HRH.

She parked directly in front of the sandstone steps, and once they were at the front door, she said, "Old money comes off differently to new, don't you think?"

Mike nodded and pressed the bell. "How the other half live, eh? I've always wanted to come here, but not like this."

A man answered. Bethany let him study her ID, and she introduced them. Maybe late thirties, early forties, he appeared relieved they were there. Whatever his age, he was distinguished, even in his casual clothes of jeans and a white polo top. He had an air about him that spoke of wealth, his brown hair cut in an old-fashioned style, his beard trimmed and neat. Short. Bright-blue eyes.

"Thank goodness you're here," he said, stepping back. "Please, do come in."

They entered and stood in a vast foyer with a marble-tiled floor, cream-coloured occasional tables, vases and ornaments on top, and a sweeping mahogany staircase directly ahead.

"I haven't heard an awful lot since my mother went missing, and I've been going out of my mind with worry." He closed the door.

"You're Harry Allthrop, yes?" Bethany asked.

"Yes, yes. Even when I telephoned for news, no one seemed to know anything much. You'd think a prominent woman going missing would cause some concern, wouldn't you?"

"It's very concerning." Bethany gazed about. "Is there somewhere we can go and sit?"

"Yes, the drawing room. Come along."

He walked off to a door and entered. Bethany and Mike followed. It was much like a living room, except it had a black grand piano and glass-fronted curio cabinets with what might be Fabergé eggs and the like inside. All expensive and beyond Bethany's pay packet.

They sat on two sofas, Bethany and Mike on one, Harry Allthrop on the other, a dark-wood coffee table between them.

"Have you heard something?" Harry asked, wringing his hands and shifting so he perched right on the edge, his knees apart.

"Tell us about your mother being missing from the beginning. When did you first notice she was gone?"

"I put Mother to bed on the Wednesday night — that's last week — like I always do. She doesn't like to go up alone, and I sit there until she's dropped off. She had her cocoa and bourbon biscuit, then off to sleep she went. It wasn't until the next morning that I found her gone. I unfortunately overslept and got up at about eleven. As you can see, this house is rather big, so I had a good few rooms to search. She sometimes wanders. Going do-lally, I'd say."

Mike gave Bethany a look that said: *Doesn't add up*.

"But your mother has been on the news and in the papers," Mike said. "She certainly seems to have all her marbles." He went on to explain. "I've followed her for years, ever since my mum told me she was royalty. She doesn't appear as though she's ageing in the brain department."

"Oh yes, royalty, that we are." Harry preened, clearly proud of his lineage.

He'd completely ignored the query about his mother's state of mind.

Mike tapped his pen on his notebook. "So you saying she's do-lally doesn't ring true for me. Just last month she cut the tape on a new charity. She spoke about what the charity was for and didn't seem in the slightest bit off."

"Oh, that's her public behaviour," Harry said, a wry expression skewing his face, one that spoke of him knowing his own mother better than Mike. "At home is a different matter. She seems to go downhill once she isn't out there doing all the things she does, so you can imagine why I'm so worried. I searched the whole house, the pool, the garage, and she wasn't there."

"Did officers come out here after you'd reported it?" Bethany asked.

"Yes, once forty-eight hours had passed, and they didn't find anything either. There was some stupid article in the paper saying she was going away for a couple of weeks to the Cotswolds. Well, I thought to myself, why would she go there without telling me? She always tells me. The police said they'd let me know if they heard of anything, but that if she's gone away for a while, perhaps for some downtime, there isn't much they can do."

Bethany nodded. "Yes, that sounds about right." Although, now that the woman's body had been found, she was a tad alarmed that nothing much had been done, but that was usually the way. With hindsight, it became clear Margaret hadn't been to the bloody Cotswolds at all, and anyway, with the area spanning over eight hundred square miles and covering five counties, that would be a hell of a lot of police involvement searching for a woman who might simply have not wanted to be found.

Now was a different matter, though.

Harry ran a hand through his hair. "They did say they'd checked cameras and hadn't spotted her car on the roads leading down to the Cotswolds, which isn't surprising as there are so many."

"I take it her car isn't here then?" Bethany said.

"No, but then again, it wouldn't be. She'd taken it to the garage for them to put on new tyres on the Wednesday and came back in a taxi."

That doesn't sound like something a do-lally woman would do.

"I see. Did you telephone the garage to see if she'd left the house on the Thursday to collect it?"

"Yes, and she hadn't. It's still there. I really should go and get it."

"No," Bethany said quickly. "We'll deal with that for you."

"Thank you, that's very kind."

"So what have you been doing in the meantime?" Bethany could have done with a coffee, but it didn't seem like this bloke would get lively and offer one.

"Ringing her friends and associates."

"Do you have a list of them?"

"I do," he said, getting up. "Come with me. I have them written down on a piece of paper on the fridge."

They followed him into a massive kitchen with all the mod cons, and he handed her the paper.

"Thanks. Mike will take a picture of that and send it to our team so they can get onto it straight away."

Mike did so while Bethany gave the room a quick once-over. Nothing seemed amiss. The work surfaces were clear apart from the usual kettle and whatnot, plus a small bowl of what resembled strawberry jam.

Harry caught where her attention had been snagged. "Oh, I'm cooking later. I have a friend coming for dinner. I need the company, not to mention a shoulder to cry on."

"I can imagine." Bethany smiled sadly. "Would you like to take a seat?" She gestured to the table and chairs.

They all went over there and got comfortable.

Still no offer of coffee.

"Would you like me to make you some tea?" she asked by way of prompting him.

"No, thank you."

That's us going drinkless then.

"This question may be distressing," Bethany said, "but do you know of anyone who would have wanted to harm your mother?"

He chuffed out a laugh, as if that suggestion was ridiculous. "No. She did a lot for the community, even going so far as to hold fetes on the grounds — well, more garden parties really, but I said fetes so you'd understand what I meant."

The cheeky bastard! Someone has a rod up his arse.

"I'm well aware of what a garden party is, sir," she said. "Us common people do have a good knowledge of things like that. Shocking, I know . . ." She let her sarcasm hang around for a beat or two, then said, "So she was a good person, yes?" She wanted to catch him out and see if he also used the past tense when referring to his mother.

An emotional cloud passed over his face for a second, then it was gone. "Oh yes, she's a good person when dealing with those less fortunate."

Hmm.

"So are you saying she *was*n't a good person to people who *are* fortunate?"

"You're twisting my words."

"I don't think so. Just asking for clarification because *your* words weren't clear. Back to the original query. Your mother wouldn't have had anyone who wanted to harm her. What about someone who might want to take her for, say, a ransom?"

His eyes lit up at that. "Do you think that's what happened? Will I get some kind of note next?"

"You haven't had any indication at all, no note, no phone call, message, or email, to give you a reason to believe someone took her?"

"No."

"Did you try calling her? I assume she had a mobile."

"Yes, she does. I rang several times. It keeps going to voicemail."

"Okay. Have you been out to look for her?"

"Yes, I've been out every day. Even just this morning."

"Where did you go?"

"To Waitrose. I stupidly thought she might be there. She always goes on a Monday. She buys the ingredients for sandwiches which she then comes home to make and takes them down to the Shadwell Women's Shelter — SWS, do you know it?"

Bethany nodded.

"They have a huge tea urn there," he said, "and she supplies the teabags, milk, and sugar. She contributes greatly with money for that place as well; she's on the board of governors."

She sounded a saint. So who would have wanted her dead? Maybe a husband of one of the women in the shelter had done her in. If she was heavily involved in it, some bloke may have found out where his wife was and blamed Margaret Allthrop for helping to provide such a place. Who the fuck knew?

After a few more questions and getting no answers to help them, Bethany gave him the news. Harry was speechless for a moment, then broke down in tears, mumbling something she couldn't understand, and when she pressed him to repeat it, he was in no fit state to comply.

With him refusing to have Alice Jacobs, the Family Liaison Officer, here to help him get over the first shock of grief, Bethany reckoned they ought to leave. Her own grief still somewhat sharp from the loss of Vinny, her husband, she had no desire to watch someone else's, bitchy as that may seem.

No, she'd had enough of the grief in her life, thank you. Harry Allthrop would just have to plod along through his, like she had to.

The ripples in the pond of death were a wicked, wicked thing, and she was just about sick of drowning.

CHAPTER THREE

Harry was impressed with the beef Wellington. The pastry had fluffed up a treat, and he'd bet the meat was pink in the middle, just as it should be. The minted new potatoes, still in their scrubbed skins, waited in a food warmer beside the butter-covered petit pois. A delicious jus completed the main meal, and now, he needed to take the potted crab starter out to Selondra along with a bottle of champers. He'd bought it all in Waitrose on his supposed trip to see if Mother was there.

Of course she fucking wasn't.

The police being here so quickly after he'd buried Mother had been a surprise. He'd expected her to remain undetected for a long while yet, and for the authorities to take ages to work out where the body was. And with him needing to get rid of all the others, things might get a little hairy. Perhaps he shouldn't have sent the letter and map for Selondra just yet. Still, he was a grieving son and no one the police needed to look at closely, although they might.

He breezed into the dining room, pushing those thoughts to the back of his mind. He carried the food on a silver tray, held aloft, as if he were Selondra's butler and not her killer. The sight of her in that black dress brought back memories of the first time he'd seen it, and he pushed them away, too.

It wasn't time to get angry yet.

He placed the food on their mats and topped up her drink in Mother's crystal flutes. Then he sat opposite Selondra at the long, shiny table that would no longer have the board members of that shitty refuge sitting around it once a week while Mother presided over them all. Once her death was common knowledge, he'd refuse to take her place on the board and would tell them he wouldn't contribute any funds in the future either. His announcement would be met with stony silence and strong glares, but he didn't care.

"Enjoy," he said. Had he sounded annoyed then? He wasn't sure.

"You're such a *whizz* in the kitchen, toots," Selondra gushed in that irritating way of hers.

"Lessons will turn anyone into a master." And he should know. Mother had sent him to the kitchen for Cook to teach him when he'd been about ten. She'd said a man who could find his way around a kitchen was a plus, and hadn't that been the truth. Once he'd hit eighteen, she'd sacked the staff, and Harry had become Cook's replacement. Harry had also become the dogsbody, and Mother had paid him a wage every week amounting to one hundred pounds. It hadn't gone up with inflation over the years. Still, he had access to the 'family' credit card if he needed anything. Mother had set it up in their joint names.

He was supposed to marry someone two decades ago, a woman Mother had approved of and arranged, but his cooking hadn't been enough to keep the young lady interested. Apparently, he was stiff and boring. She'd laughed at him, just like Selondra. If only he'd managed to get away from Mother back then, things might have turned out differently. He most certainly wouldn't be sitting here waiting for the right moment to kill Selondra. Perhaps he'd have had children and would be so caught up in them that Mother's behaviour towards him might have changed. If it had, he wouldn't have felt the need to get rid of her.

Move along . . .

The meal was underway with delicate scrapes of silver cutlery on china plates, and they ate and talked about Selondra's 'shitty-shit-shit' day — "Oh, *such* a disaster, darling!" — where she'd shouted at the nail technician for using the wrong shade of pink and bitten the head off her hairdresser for cutting more than the instructed inch. Demanded more like. Selondra didn't usually ask those types of people nicely. They were minions to her, there to do her bidding.

He'd met her via Mother. Selondra liked to do her bit at the refuge, too.

Much later, the main course surpassed her requirements, so she said. "I'm *sooo* hankering for the brulée, Harry. Your desserts are to die for."

He smiled and stood, collecting the dinner plates. "Yes, they're to die for. I'll just go and get them."

Leaving her to sip yet more champagne — she must have three quarters of the bottle sloshing around inside her, the greedy bugger — he went into the kitchen. The dishes could wait, so he popped them on the worktop beside the large knife he'd be using later. He'd named it My Gorgeous. The blade gleamed from the overhead lights, winking at him, letting him know it was as excited as he was to use it.

"There, there," he said, stroking the handle. "Not long to wait now."

Desserts and spoons on the tray, complete with a glass dish of the strawberry and arse-flesh preserve, he joined her in the dining room.

"Oh my *God*," she said, over-the-top, her ridiculous, drawn-on eyebrows rising high. "That looks *divine*. Such a shame we're not compatible in bed, otherwise you'd be a keeper."

"About that . . ." Now was the time to lure her in, get her to think he wanted to know how to have sex 'properly'. "I want you to teach me."

"Excuse me?" She hiccoughed and giggled at the same time. "You want me to *teach* you?"

Why had she repeated that? It wasn't like she hadn't bloody heard him correctly.

She wafted a hand, her nails bright pink, a lighter shade of the preserve sitting on her spoon that hovered in front of her mouth. "I haven't got the inclination to show you the ropes. And like I said before, why don't you watch some of that saucy stuff, those films where people go at it like animals? That'll give you a head start."

Porn. Dreadful. He'd never wanted to watch anything less. The magazines and 'toy' he'd bought after that awful night with Selondra had almost sent him rushing to the toilet to vomit. "Oh, I thought . . ."

"Oh, Harry . . ."

The image of her sporting a second smile on her neck flashed through his mind. "Please? Just one session."

"Session! What a romantic you are." She threw her head back and laughed, exposing that neck.

The one he wanted to slash right this second or stab with a cake fork.

Why was she laughing? *At* him? Or because of what he'd said? He could never be sure with her. "What's so funny?"

She paused, hand to her throat, and he wondered for a silly moment whether she had an inkling what was going to happen and was shielding it for when My Gorgeous bit it.

"Oh, you're such an incompetent fool." She smiled, as if that would take the sting out of her words.

It didn't.

"How have you got through life so far?" she said. "Thirty-nine years, and you've not mastered sex. Have you been living under a rock?"

No, just here. With Mother. "Something like that. Please don't laugh at my expense."

She sobered, perhaps taking note of the steel in his tone. "Okay, one session."

I wasn't expecting her to say yes . . .

"I need you to be naked before we start," he said.

"Oh, different to last time, when you molested me without me having a chance to get undressed. I'd only managed to get my knickers off, and there you were — or there 'it' was — prodding at me. I had to explain it might be nice to be nude, remember?"

"Is that wrong, what I did?"

Mother had told him sex was for procreation, none of that pleasure business Selondra had asked him to give her.

"Just get to her hole," Mother had said. "Shove it in there."

"It's not wrong if that's your thing," Selondra said. "Nothing is so long as it isn't hurting anyone and it's consensual. But most people tend to explore bodies a bit when they're, you know, doing it." She ate some jam.

Yes . . .

"I see." Perhaps he should try that. He might like it, although he doubted it. When he'd been with prostitutes, they'd encouraged him not to touch, and that had become the norm for him. He hadn't even been allowed to kiss them. It apparently wasn't on the list of things they did. Strange then, that they'd offered to suck him *down there*. That was far dirtier than having a kiss. "So will you take your clothes off?"

"What, now?" She gaped, gesturing at the room. "Shouldn't we go to the bedroom first?"

"No," he said, a little too quickly. "It has to be here."

"Do you have some hidden kinks I'm not aware of?"

No, he didn't, but if they went upstairs, My Gorgeous wouldn't be close enough for him to go and get her. Selondra would see him with it before he wanted her to if he went to grab the knife on their way up there. Now, he'd have to pretend he knew more than he really did in order to keep her in this room. "You can sit in this chair with a blindfold on."

That had sounded plausible. Lots of people used those. Mother had told him stories about that, how men and women liked whips and all manner of things while being nude. She'd gone into great detail, and he'd been uncomfortable listening as she'd spewed out words that had altered his perception. He'd been schooled at home, hadn't been allowed to mix with anyone other than the children of her friends. Sequestered away, with no television, his experience of the outside world was limited until he'd hit adulthood, and by then, he was so brainwashed by her, he hadn't had the desire to find out things for himself outside of these walls — until he'd reached thirty and, despite her threatening to disinherit him like she always had, he'd gone against her and learnt a bit about the world beyond what she'd told him.

New things. Scary things. And exciting things.

When she'd died, he'd bought a TV. There would be filthy things on there, no doubt, things that could corrupt, and he didn't want to view them. He'd have to find something nice to watch. Maybe *Thomas the Tank Engine*. To have a smart phone had been a revelation these past few days, although he'd used Mother's on past occasions when she'd asked him to.

"A blindfold?" Selondra all but shrieked. "Now you're talking my language."

"It's not a proper blindfold. Just one of my ties."

"That'll do."

She stripped then, fast and without finesse, none of that 'charming' business Mother had told him to watch out for, like men did to snakes in baskets. A striptease. Something to lure him into the woman's web. He had to watch out for that. Females had a habit of taking advantage.

Selondra stood there, hands on hips, head cocked. "Your tie?"

He blinked to force himself to stop staring at her body. "Yes, my tie." He took it off and walked towards her. "Sit there."

She did, opening her legs wide, and Harry gawped at the procreation hole, wanting to shove it in like Mother had said and make a baby. But he couldn't. Not with Selondra. She'd upset him in the past and had to suffer the consequences, just like all the others would.

He covered her eyes with the tie and secured it at the back of her head, then turned to get the brulée. He spooned some into her mouth, ensuring the preserve was the main thing on there.

"Ooh," she said. "That is so good, although I'm not sure about the crystallised bits."

The arse.

He clamped his lips to stop his laughter coming out.

She chewed, and he gazed, fascinated that she was eating Mother's bottom.

"What does it taste like?" he asked then held his breath while he scooped more onto the spoon.

"It's a bit meaty if I'm honest. Give me some more."

He did, and she swirled it over her tongue again.

"Don't go anywhere," he said. "I need to get something."

"Oh, you tease!"

He went into the kitchen, snapped on some gloves — didn't want to get blood on his hands — and picked up My Gorgeous, which he buffed with a tea towel. Back in the dining room, he approached Selondra, already eager to slice her neck, but that would have to wait until they were in the appropriate location.

Placing My Gorgeous on another chair, he then guided Selondra to her feet and whispered, "I want you on the table."

"Good grief! What's got into you?" she said. "Not that I'm complaining."

He helped her onto it and ordered her to rest facedown. With rope from the sideboard, he tied the ends around her wrists and ankles, much to her amusement. Then he knotted the other ends together beneath the table so she was strapped tight and couldn't move anything but her head.

"What are you up to?" she asked, her voice holding a tinge of fear along with curiosity.

"You'll see."

Then he grabbed My Gorgeous. Hovered the blade over Selondra's backside.

And sliced off her arse cheek.

* * *

"Your father was a horrible man," Mother said, circling Harry at his desk.

She'd told him to answer questions on the task sheet about To Kill a Mockingbird, *but they eluded him. While she was in this kind of mood, his brain cells concentrated on what she said, not his schoolwork, him waiting for something awful to happen.*

"Yes, a vile man. You only have sex to make a baby. Repeat that, Harry."

He did, and she patted him on the head.

"Good boy. Now, unfortunately, you're to play with Delilah Baynard's children this afternoon. She insists on coming by to discuss the refuge. Remember, do not listen to anything those boys tell you. They're somewhat corrupt, and you're pure. I don't want them tainting you."

Mrs Baynard was one of the other ladies on the refuge board of governors, a rich sort, although not as rich as Mother. She also gave a lot of time and money to the women who needed to stay there, ensuring they were safe from 'wicked husbands' or 'vile men'.

Harry was ushered into the nursery, which was more of a playroom now, and told to await the arrival of Tobias and Charles Baynard. He loved them coming over because he got to feel like a real boy. They clattered in, all gangly legs and smelling of fresh air, and set to playing with his toy cars.

After a while, Tobias whispered, "I saw someone's boobs today."

Charles pitched into a fit of giggles. "So did I."

Harry contemplated them. "What are boobs?"

Tobias roared, too. "You don't know what boobs are? They're titties."

"I don't know what that is either." Harry's cheeks got a bit too warm. They itched.

"These," Tobias said, clutching his chest and jiggling. "Except on ladies."

Oh. Breasts. Mother had told him about those. They held milk for babies and weren't to be used for anything else. That was why women had bras. They were for hiding them in.

"Why would you want to see those?" Harry asked.

"Because that's what boys like. And we saw her minnie."

"Her what?"

"That thing between her legs," Charles said. "It was all hairy."

The lads all but wet themselves, and Harry squirmed, uncomfortable with this kind of talk. If Mother found out, he'd be in so much trouble, and his friends wouldn't be allowed here anymore.

"Shh," he said. "If Mother hears you . . ."

"Oh, neither of them will. They were downstairs drinking wine when we came up."

At eight years old, Harry knew what true fear was. He knew so many other things these boys didn't know, and he envied them.

"We took a picture with Father's Polaroid," Tobias said, whipping the image out and shoving it under Harry's nose. "Look at it."

Harry scrunched his eyes closed. Even though Mother wasn't there, he couldn't peek. She'd know, and he'd be punished for being a 'vile man' in the making.

"No," he said. "Don't make me see it."

"Open your eyes, otherwise we'll tell our mother you touched our willies."

Harry wanted to cry. He was stuck between obeying them and obeying Mother. Which was worse? Seeing the picture and Mother finding out about it, or her thinking he'd touched their private parts?

He opened his eyes, confronted with the breasts and minnie. "Oh . . ." He didn't know what else to say. Then, "Who is that?"

"One of the maids," Charles said. "She has to use the pool because of her sore back, and Father allowed it. He sometimes sits and watches her swim — and she never has any clothes on!"

The brothers laughed again.

Harry held back tears.

"Who never has any clothes on?" Mother said.

Harry glared at Tobias, willing him to put the photo away. Then he turned. Mother stood in the nursery doorway, glaring at them all one after the other.

"The maid." That was Delilah, standing behind her. "Frank has a penchant for her."

Mother swivelled to face her friend. "Oh, that's disgraceful talk in front of the children."

"Why? They're going to be just the same when they grow up." Delilah fluffed her hair.

"Not my son," Mother swung round to point at Tobias and Charles. "Out. Go downstairs and wait until your mother is ready to leave. Harry, go to The Study."

It wasn't a study but a bare room where he had to 'study' his behaviour and only come out when he'd realised the error of his ways.

He waited for Charles and Tobias to leave the nursery, the pair of them giggling and pulling faces behind Mother's back as she led them along the landing, Delilah taking the lead. At the top of the stairs, the boys held their chests like Tobias had earlier, then shrieked.

"Stop it, you filthy children," Mother said.

They all disappeared, and Harry made his way to The Study. Inside, he closed the door and went to the window to peer out. Milton, the gardener, was out there tending to the weeds. He must have sensed Harry watching; he glanced up and waved.

Harry waved back, a caged bird, and wished he could break out of there and fly away.

He couldn't, though. Mother had clipped his wings.

CHAPTER FOUR

Bethany sat beside Mike on her sofa, tummy full of meat feast pizza. Her size sixteen thighs had shrivelled to a twelve in the three months since Vinny's death, and she didn't like it. Vinny had preferred her carrying a bit of weight, and no matter how much she tried to get back to her previous size, mourning had a mind to keep it off.

They'd spent the evening talking about the case, and Mike had given her a lesson in who Margaret Allthrop was, going back in time on the internet and showing her pictures. Harry Allthrop didn't feature in any of the images or articles, and tomorrow, Fran and Leona could get on with poking farther into his background to see if something dodgy came up. Bethany didn't expect anything except for an education at Eton or some such place. Bethany and Mike had finished for the day once they'd left him, Bethany messaging Fran to tell them to go home, too, and that whatever they'd found could wait until the morning.

Mike stayed over a lot these days, especially since Bethany had moved out of the house she'd bought with Vinny and into a ground-floor flat that had a nice garden only she used — when she had the bloody time. A new area, he'd said, meant he had to keep an eye on her until she'd settled in properly.

It was what Vinny would have expected of him, so that was fine by her. Plus, she had a feeling Mike wanted to look after her while she segued into her new home, hanging around so he could be there if she broke down. He hadn't had a girlfriend since his last one had walked out on him, so maybe he could do with the company, too. Whatever, their coexistence worked.

These walls didn't hold many memories yet, they were there ready to soak up her future life, and she'd dropped Vinny's clothing off at one of those bank things in the supermarket car park. It had been hard to let go, but she had to. She'd been going mad, smelling Vinny, imagining him wearing the jumpers and T-shirts, pressing them to her face and sniffing.

Tears burned, so she plunged into conversation.

"The son is off," she said, putting her plate on the coffee table, throwing her thoughts out of her head. "Even though he didn't say anything questionable, he's on my radar. What did you think?"

"I'm more for that John Cribbins bloke at the wind farm."

"Why?"

"I don't know, but he was shifty."

"I'll give you that, and I do think he's involved, but why would he kill Margaret Allthrop?"

"Why does anyone kill anybody?"

"There is that. Fancy a glass of wine or a beer?"

"A beer," he said. "Thanks."

She went to pick up the plates, but he beat her to it.

"You're not to wait on me. I'm a mate, not a proper guest," he said. "Bugger off and get the drinks while I sort this lot."

She walked into the kitchen and took a bottle of Becks and white wine from the fridge. Mike loaded the dishwasher, a slim effort she'd had installed, seeing as her normal one wouldn't have fitted. The rest of the flat was spacious, but the kitchen was a bit on the slender side. A galley. Not that it mattered. For the most part there was only her to fit in it, and

Mike knew her so well that when he was there, he dodged out of her way while she cooked. Which wasn't often. Work hindered culinary efforts.

She carried the drinks into the living room and plonked herself down, staring through the window at the row of houses opposite. A streetlamp cast an orange glow over the parked cars, and she wondered whether the neighbours thought she and Mike were a couple. That'd be a fun conversation if they ever asked.

The man in question came back and lifted the remote, raising his eyebrows. "Film?"

"Go on then. Something light, though. None of that murder shit you like. I've had enough of that for one day."

He sat and selected Netflix, choosing something or other with Jennifer Aniston and a dog in it.

"Uh, that's meant to make you cry," she said. "So it can fuck off."

"Shit, sorry." He flicked through a few more and opted for *The Hangover*.

"Christ." She shook her head. "I'm going to read instead, but you carry on."

It wasn't long before her eyes drooped and she dozed off, Kindle in hand.

* * *

Fran and Leona were already at work when Bethany and Mike arrived.

"Morning!" Bethany called, dumping her jacket on the coat rack by the door then going over to make herself and Mike a coffee. "We need to poke into Harry Allthrop's past."

"Already did that yesterday," Leona said, pointing to the whiteboard.

Of course, Bethany and Mike hadn't returned to the station after they'd visited Harry, and she'd just told them to go home. She made the coffees, handed one to Mike, then went over to read the information.

Harry Allthrop, thirty-nine, an only child. Mother now deceased, his father dead, too, when Harry was about five. Heart attack. Harry wasn't down as attending mainstream school but taught at home. He'd passed his GCSE exams with flying colours, all A marks, but he'd never been employed.

"That's weird," she said over her shoulder.

"What is?" Leona asked.

"Harry not having a job. Ever." Bethany frowned.

"Well, he is posh. Maybe he doesn't need to work," Fran said. "Although he has a bank account. Want me to put in for the paperwork to have a nose at it?"

"Please. It won't hurt to see what's going on there. He might have paid out a lump sum for services rendered, if you catch my drift. Pop along to see Kribbs and ask him to sort it for you." She sighed. Ordinarily, she'd go and ask the chief herself, but he was still acting weird, mentioning his health issues but not going into detail about it. Whatever it was, it didn't affect his work, although he did seem to hobble sometimes. Just as well he was a desk jockey then. She didn't fancy getting embroiled in his personal affairs; she had enough of her own to contend with.

Bethany continued reading the board. Margaret Allthrop had a net worth of around four million, a strong reason to have her killed if you stood to inherit, although surely Harry wouldn't be that dim. He was the only family member left, according to the info, so suspicion was bound to fall on him as the one to have either committed the crime or finding someone else to do it. Margaret's other relatives had died over the past few years, one after the other, which could seem suss if their manners of death weren't ordinary. All in all, jack shit to go on, as usual. Unless she counted the theft of the borer. That was the route she'd have to take. It had to lead somewhere.

"Okay." She turned to face her team, waiting for Fran to sit at her desk since she'd just come back in from seeing Kribbs. "Paperwork on the go?"

"Yes," Fran said. "Do you know what's up with him? He yelped when he got up from his desk."

"No idea," Bethany said. "Maybe he trod on a drawing pin. Right, I need you on CCTV this morning, again on all roads leading to and from the one where the body dump site is, plus the ones around Shadwell Wind Energy. I know you had a look yesterday, but I'm convinced that missing borer made that hole. Where is that borer now? Who owns the genny that fired it up? Who used the borer? These are questions we need answers to, and you can guarantee it'll lead us closer to whoever killed Margaret Allthrop. Now, with all her family dead apart from her son, we need to poke some more into friends and associates. As we know, she helped run the local women's refuge, SWS. Did a disgruntled husband or partner take umbrage at Margaret for her part in the place? Had someone previously contacted her with regards to finding his wife or girlfriend, and Margaret had sent him on his way with his tail between his legs? Or did someone on the refuge board have it in for her and decided she needed offing?"

She paused to take a sip of coffee. That was where she'd go next, actually, to the refuge to chat to the staff and women there, get some idea of what they thought of Margaret. The governors would need talking to an' all, so she'd best get cracking.

"Mike, if you can send that picture to Fran and Leona, the one you took of Margaret's list of friends, that'd be great."

"I did that yesterday after I took the picture," he said.

"Shit, so you did."

"We began going through them but didn't manage to finish," Fran said.

"Okay, continue that then, as well as CCTV. How is Facebook and the like coming on?"

"She's only on Facebook. Got a fan page that doubles up as her mouthpiece," Leona said. "She puts up pictures of her attending functions, plus there are links to self-help places for battered women if there's no room at the one in Shadwell. She seems to have been a staunch advocate of women's rights, pushing for laws to be passed regarding domestic abuse and restraining orders — there's a post where she says about orders not protecting the women. Their exes have to actually harm them, or the victims need proof of threats before anything is done."

Bethany nodded. "Well, we all know how that works out, and we're just as frustrated as she was about that. I've always wondered what good a restraining order would be when a lot of the people they're issued to bloody ignore them and approach or harass folks anyway."

"She was trying to get that changed. There's a petition going." Fran sighed. "Makes you wonder if she suffered abuse herself and that's why she felt so strongly about it. Shall I look into that as well?"

"Yes, please." Bethany nodded. "Right, Mike, we need to get down to that refuge, then we could have a quick stop at Shadwell Wind Energy and see if it rattles John Cribbins when we turn up again. Oh, he needs looking into as well." She scratched her head. "Shit, that's a lot of work for you to be getting on with. Want me to draft in some extra hands?"

Leona tapped her temple with a pen. "Hmm, we kind of don't trust anyone else to get on with it properly."

"I know what you mean. Okay, do your thing, but if you get overwhelmed, ring down to Rob on the front desk and see if he can source you a couple of people from the other teams — doesn't matter what they specialise in, we just want eyes on Facebook and CCTV while you do all the other stuff."

"Will do." Leona spun to face her monitor.

Bethany jerked her head at Mike, and they left the station to drive to the refuge, based on the outskirts of Shadwell. It was a house much like Harry Allthrop now owned — providing Margaret had left it to him — but shabbier, weather-beaten, the windows in need of a good paint, although the panes were clean. A high stone wall surrounded the property, and a wrought-iron gate shut the world out at the end of a long tarmac driveway.

"Press that intercom thing there, will you?" she asked Mike.

He opened his window and reached out to jab at a button on a silver pole.

"How may I help you?" a woman said, her voice crackly through a hidden speaker.

"DS Mike Wilkins and DI Bethany Smith. We need to speak to the owner about Margaret Allthrop," he said.

"Drive closer to the gate and show your ID, please." The woman sounded like she didn't believe who they were.

A camera perched on top of the wall ahead, the lens glaring at them. She nudged the car forward a bit and held her ID up out of the window, as did Mike. Not that whoever was looking would see it clearly.

"Ring the station," Mike shouted back at the pole. "We'll wait."

A couple of minutes passed, then a buzz went off. The gate swung inwards, and Bethany shot off up the drive, glancing in her rearview. The gate had already closed, and she wondered whether that had been designed so only one vehicle could get through at once. A good safety measure if angry exes loitered about.

She parked up around the side where other cars were, and they were met by a blonde woman, skinny, her jeans even skinnier, a pink T-shirt painted on, boobs straining against the material. She had her arms folded, and goosebumps littered her skin from the cold air. Fluffy baby-pink slippers engulfed her small feet.

Bethany and Mike showed their IDs again.

"Hi, I'm Diana, the daytime warden. I came here for help years ago and ended up staying. They gave me a job. Come this way."

Bit of a speech when first meeting someone.

Diana led them towards a black-painted wooden door, ivy creeping up the dark-grey stones around it. Inside, she waited for them to enter the magnolia-painted corridor then locked up. "Can't be too careful. There's a nutter about at the moment."

"A nutter?" Bethany asked as they walked on.

"Yes," Diana said over her shoulder. "Keeps ringing up with threats. Is that why you're here, to talk to Margaret about it? Only, she's missing, so her son said, and we're worried that the man who keeps ringing has done something to her. He was nasty last time. Told Margaret he'd slice off her arse cheek."

What? Bethany thought about Margaret's backside in the grave. "Oh, that *is* nasty." *Oh my bloody God!* "How long has he been calling for?"

"About a month or so." She stopped outside a door at the end. "Let's go into my office so the women don't hear. We haven't said anything to them. They have enough to worry about without us piling on more."

While Mike followed Diana in, Bethany peered around the corridor corner. A large living area contained several sofas and chairs, coffee tables, bookcases stuffed with novels and DVDs, and two children played on a rug while a woman read, her legs tucked up under her.

In the office now, Bethany took a seat next to Mike in front of the desk. Diana sat behind it, drawing a diary towards her.

"We've been writing it all down, like the police told us to," Diana said. "Whoever it is doesn't stay on the line for long, and we were informed nothing much could be done anyway. We got hold of BT, and they set up a caller display thing, and we bought all new phones with the windows on them so we can see who's calling, but of course, the fucker blocked his number."

"Probably using a pay-as-you-go anyway," Mike said.

Diana huffed. "Whatever he's using, it's scaring us now that Margaret is missing. What's going on?"

"I'm afraid Margaret's body was found yesterday," Bethany said.

"Her *body*?" Diana's eyes widened, and she slapped a hand over her mouth. "She's *dead*?"

"Yes. Sorry to drop that news on you then ask questions, but we need build a picture of who Margaret was — the Margaret not in the limelight. Do you feel up to telling us about her?"

Diana nodded, lowering her hand. "She's lovely. You wouldn't think she's posh at all. She treats us all the same, very welcoming and caring. She was the first person I saw when I arrived here. I'd escaped a terrible marriage — thank God I didn't have any kids with him — and Margaret showed me to my room and told me the rules. She's a bit weird with some of her ways, but you get used to them."

"Weird ways?" Mike wrote that down.

"Well, she thinks sex is only for procreation and that all men are 'vile beasts'." Diana smiled sadly. "There's no telling her that not every male is an arsehole, even though her son is a nice man."

Bethany perked up. "You know Harry then?"

"Oh yes, he helps here sometimes. Margaret makes lush lunches, and he comes with her to carry it all in and set it up. We're kind of friends."

"Do you know where he works?" Mike asked.

"At home. He looks after the house and grounds. Margaret says he enjoys it, and she pays him a wage. I suppose it saves employing loads of people if Harry can do it. Their place is massive. Have you seen it?"

Bethany nodded. At least they'd got an explanation for why Harry had never worked. She wickedly wondered why he wasn't paying tax — there was no record of him having done so.

"Mind you, I think it's something ridiculous like a hundred quid a week." Diana shrugged. "Hardly much for the amount he does."

That explained the tax angle then. He didn't earn enough to pay any. But did he have a beef with his mother about the low wage, amongst other things? They'd have to go back and speak to him, ask questions about his life, get some sort of idea how he felt about the world in general, gauging what kind of person he was. He hadn't let much slip when they'd seen him before.

"What does he do then?" Bethany asked.

Diana rubbed her temples. "Gardening, cooking, cleaning. Everything."

"I see. So they're both nice people?"

"Definitely. This will crush Harry. She's all he really knows. As far as I've made out, he doesn't have a social life as such, no friends — well, not unless you count me and Selondra, but that relationship went down the shitter anyway, so discount that."

"Who is Selondra?"

"She volunteers here. Donates plus comes in to play with the kids, giving the mothers a break. She's great with the children, too. She was seeing Harry for a bit — a few meals at the big house, some in the city — but he wasn't her cup of tea in the end."

"Did she say why?" Bethany needed to know if Harry had it in him to kill, so an insight into his private life might shed some light.

"I'd rather not say." Diana blushed.

"It's all right, it's only us. We won't be telling anyone what you said. We'll need to speak to Selondra anyway, so she'll have to answer the same questions." Bethany smiled, impatience nipping at her.

"He was, well, shit in bed," Diana said. "Wham, bam, that sort of fella."

How wonderful . . .

Bethany asked Diana if they could use her office to speak to all the staff and residents — apart from the children — and once everyone had been in, each person saying Margaret and Harry were exemplary people, Bethany just had one more person to interview.

"Selondra?" she said to Diana when the last person had gone.

"Oh, she's not in today. I gave her a ring intending to ask her to nip by, but she's not answering — her mobile and landline go to voicemail."

"Is that unusual?"

Diana laughed. "No. She could be getting her nails or hair done, having a massage. Selondra comes from money, so she's usually off getting pampered in one form or another."

"When did you last see Harry?" Bethany asked.

"Yesterday. I went round there for a cuppa. Harry needed someone to talk to, you know, about his mum disappearing."

"Didn't he tell you about her death?" Bethany frowned.

"No. Hmm, strange."

It was, considering he'd told them he was having a friend round for a shoulder to cry on. Was that Diana or someone else? If Diana, why hadn't he told her? Saying that, Bethany could understand why. Since losing Vinny, she'd had countless people offering to help her by talking through it, but she hadn't been able to face it. Maybe Harry was the same. Perhaps he'd planned to spill his guts to Diana or his dinner guest, but when it had come to it, he couldn't.

"Well, thanks for letting us take up so much of your day." It was closing in on one o'clock. The interviews had scoffed the whole bloody morning. "But we must be off now. I'll get on to someone at the station about those phone calls. If you can give me the number he's calling you on, that will help."

Diana handed over a card. "Thanks."

"Can you also give me Selondra's number and address?"

Diana fished around for a business card and handed it out. In bold lettering: SELONDRA IMES, LIVE LIFE TO THE FULL.

Okay . . .

With goodbyes said, she showed them out the way they'd come in.

In the car, Bethany said, "If he's clever, he'll be using several burners, so getting hold of BT for the numbers that called will probably be useless if he's ditched them."

"But it might not be," Mike said. "The mobiles will have pinged towers. We might be able to find out who bought them and where."

"True."

“When she said the man mentioned cutting off arse cheeks, I almost said ‘shit’.” Mike shook his head.

She sighed. “You and me both. Yep, we need to get that refuge number checked out. It’ll hopefully lead us straight to the sick bastard.”

CHAPTER FIVE

John Cribbins was crapping himself. The sodding police were here again, yakking to Vellord down the other end of the room. What did they want? To speak to him? He'd fucked up last time, acting shifty, and he swore they didn't believe that he'd been at the Shank. But he *had* been there, all night, he'd made sure of it, just so he'd be spotted.

He'd put the borer by the door so whoever had come to get it didn't have to hang about. He'd also snipped the bloody CCTV wires, and that had come to light this morning when the security company had finally turned up. Vellord suspected everyone who worked there now, and John would bet he was telling those coppers all about it right this second.

Shit.

John faked working on his computer, just so he didn't appear on edge, but he was and didn't think he could hide it for much longer. The five hundred quid he'd been given for doing those two little jobs had gone, spent on a mortgage payment because he'd got so behind since Gina had upped and left him. Gambling would do that, stop you paying bills — and without anyone to care for you. It was a habit he'd broken once, for Gina, but since his dad had died, John had slipped back into it. The sounds of the fruit machines were always a comfort.

Fuck. Those detectives were coming over. He studied their reflection in his monitor and let out a long, shaky breath. He was going to have to confess at this rate. His heart was doing a number on him, all pitter-pattery, and his body went cold like it did whenever he lost a ton of money in the slots.

"Mr Cribbins . . ." The woman.

He didn't like her. She gazed at you like she knew things, and as for the bloke, he glared right into your soul, the unnerving bastard. Or maybe that was guilt talking.

John spun round on his stool and smiled. "Hello again."

"We nipped into the Shank on our way here," she said.

No hello. No smile. What a strange mare. Smith. That was her name, wasn't it? He thought it was anyway. Relief settled inside him despite her demeanour. They'd have found out he was at the pub, like he'd said. Nothing to worry about here.

"Have a pint or two, did you?" he said. Stupid. Such a stupid thing to say.

"Um, not likely while we're on duty, is it," she said and gave him a funny look.

What she didn't add was, "You fucking plonker." He reckoned she'd thought it, though.

"The manager there seems to know you well," she went on, casting aspersions about the amount of time he spent there.

Like it's any of her business.

With Gina gone, what else was there for him to do except twiddle his thumbs at home in front of the TV while resisting the flashing lights of a slotty, the lure of putting pound after pound in it, hoping to double his money?

John reddened. "I'm there quite a bit."

"So he said. You like the fruit machines." She tapped her foot. Judging.

"So what if I do? No crime, is it?"

"None at all," she said. "So what we now need to do is establish what time you got home. The Shank manager said you left about ten past eleven."

"I walked home, and it isn't far, so I'd have got back about twenty past."

"You told us before that you'd stayed home from eleven onwards."

Bugger it. "What's twenty minutes?"

"Quite a lot. In that time, someone could steal a borer."

"Now hang on a bleedin' second." John's heart thundered, and the tips of his ears burned hot. "I didn't steal anything."

"I didn't say you did." She smiled. "I said *someone*. You're a bit tetchy for an 'innocent' man."

"Yeah, well, you're trying to mess with my head, that's what you're doing. I didn't take the fucking borer, all right?" Not a lie. Christ, he was getting in a tizz. *Calm down.*

"No need to be arsey, Mr Cribbins, we're just doing our job."

"And I'm just doing mine. Or trying to anyway," he muttered.

"We'll be speaking to your neighbours next," she said. "See if they saw or heard what time you got home."

"Be my guest." He shrugged. That was better, going for nonchalant. "I went straight home after the Shank. Told you that before."

"Maybe we'll speak to Uncle Crack as well, because you mentioned he'd seen you."

God, why the hell did I say that?

Her sly grin was getting right on his nips. If they spoke to Crack and found out John had bought a little baggie of something that night, they might tell Vellord. John would lose his job. Vellord had a no-drugs policy, even if it was for recreation. A bit of weed didn't hurt anybody, but the boss wouldn't see it that way.

John had smoked a fat joint that night then conked out, waking up in the morning on the sofa.

He shrugged again. "Do what you have to. No skin off my nose."

"What's your take on the borer theft?" she asked.

He hadn't been expecting that. "Dunno. They can dig down about four or five metres, so your guess is as good as mine as to why anyone would need a hole that big. Maybe they were building a well." Another stupid answer. He was full of them today.

"Do you know anyone who would want to build a well?"

She was baiting him, waiting for him to slip up. Did she know stuff and was just playing with him?

"Nope," he said.

"If you knew of anyone, you'd say, wouldn't you?" she asked. "Because the longer people hide the truth, the worse it ends up for them. If they speak now, it's less of a charge, and helping the police, well, it makes the secret keeper look better."

"That's their problem then, isn't it, not mine." *Secret keeper. She bloody knows.* "Now, can I get back to work?" He turned to face his screen.

"Have a nice day, Mr Cribbins."

He watched them march off in the monitor reflection, his arsehole spasming through fear. Convinced those two knew what he'd done, he struggled to concentrate. He'd have to get hold of his friend and make sure the bloke didn't spill as to John's involvement. He shouldn't have done what he had in the first place, but he'd been desperate for money.

Pissing hell!

CHAPTER SIX

"What do you think?" Bethany asked Mike in the car as they sped off towards Cribbins' address.

"He's hiding something, I know that much. Got guilt written all over him."

"I agree. We'll nip to his street and ask a few questions, although the Shank manager was certain Cribbins had been there that night because of the darts — it had stuck in his mind. Plus, he'd shaken hands with Crack, and we all know what that means."

"Hmm. He might well have been there and gone home but could have also left again to steal the borer. Did Fran get back to you on what vehicle Cribbins owns?"

Bethany had texted her for that information before they'd gone into Wind Energy. "Have a look at my phone for me, will you? I put it on silent so we weren't disturbed." She got it out of her pocket and passed it over. "He'd need a van. That borer is pretty big, although I wonder how it cuts into the ground?"

"Weren't you listening to Vellord?" Mike swiped her phone screen.

"Um, I was too busy watching Cribbins. He was sitting stiff as a bloody board."

"Vellord said it has an extending cutter, like a telescope. They set the machine to whatever depth they want, then it does the job. Right, it says here that Cribbins has a Ford Mondeo. Never owned a van in his life."

"So? He might have borrowed one. Can you message Fran and ask her to look into his friends, see what vehicles are registered to them? We need to get some lunch first. It's two-fifteen now, for God's sake. We'll stop at the local shops near Cribbins'."

Mike sent the message. "I'll recap in case you missed the whole convo. According to Vellord, someone snipped the CCTV wires. Got to be an inside job, seeing as the footage stopped about four in the afternoon."

"But like he said, employees are free to access all areas — yep, I did hear that bit. It could have been any one of them. I'll stop in this shop here. What do you fancy?"

"A meal deal — sandwich, crisps, and a drink. Surprise me. Thanks."

She parked, got what she needed in the shop, then returned to the car. They ate without talking for a while, then Bethany jolted at the sight of Cuppa, Vinny's fireman colleague/friend, getting out of his Kia and walking towards the shop.

She dipped her head, staring at the last quarter of her ploughman's baguette.

Mike nudged her. "Isn't that . . . ?"

"It is."

"Don't you want to . . . ?"

"Nope."

She started the engine and drove off, irrational panic fluttering inside her. She didn't feel up to seeing Cuppa — or anyone who viewed her with sympathy in their eyes. He'd ask how she was coping without Vinny and offer to come and see her for one of those cuppas that had earned him his nickname. He'd been the one to call her on that dreadful night Vinny had been caught in a fire, and she knew damn well she was avoiding the messenger so she didn't shoot him.

She'd avoided him at the funeral, too, except to allow him to say 'sorry', like so many others had done.

Sorry wasn't an adequate word to show empathy when someone had died. *No* words were enough to describe the feeling of utter helplessness, loneliness, and desperation that grief plummeted you into.

Was she a bitch for driving off like this? Cuppa would only be concerned for her — he'd messaged her numerous times over the last couple of months, but she hadn't returned them, preferring to bury her head in the sand and carry on as though none of it had happened. Pretending Vinny was off somewhere on a long course that just happened to last the rest of her life.

"One day, grief's going to come calling properly and slap you silly," Mike said. "You can't keep bottling it all up."

"It's the only way for me to cope. Work. You know that. I'm doing it for Vinny. He'd want me to keep going, not be moping about, and anyway, I do a fair bit of that when I'm on my own. Just because you don't always see me flailing doesn't mean I don't do it from time to time. Believe me, it swallows me up until I can't fucking breathe. I just . . . I don't know. Cuppa will want to tell stories and reminisce about Vinny. I don't want to. It'll hurt too much, and I'm not ready for that bollocks, all right?" She parked outside Cribbins' house. "And . . . saved by the bell." She took her phone off Mike and scanned her messages.

> Fran: WE'VE GONE THROUGH CRIBBINS' FACEBOOK FRIENDS, DONE VEHICLES, AND NONE OWN A VAN.

> Bethany: OKAY, THANKS. ANYTHING ELSE FOR ME?

> Fran: NOTHING ON CCTV. YOU MIGHT WANT TO VISIT A WOMAN WHO USED TO BE A COOK FOR THE ALLTHROPS,

THOUGH. I JUST GOT OFF THE PHONE WITH HER, AND YOU HAVE TO HEAR WHAT SHE HAS TO SAY. NOREEN WITHERS. NINETEEN JILLBELL DRIVE.

Bethany: OKAY. WE'RE QUICKLY ASKING CRIBBINS' NEIGHBOURS A FEW QUESTIONS, THEN WE'LL GO THERE. CATCH YOU LATER.

"Right, just the immediate neighbours," she said to Mike. "I'll fire off a quick message to Rob to ask him to get a uniform down here to question all the rest. We have somewhere else we need to be."

"Where's that?" Mike unclipped his seat belt.

Bethany jabbed at her text screen. "A woman who used to work for Margaret. She's got what I can only imagine is some gossip for us."

Message sent, they got out of the car and took two houses each either side of Cribbins' place. No one had seen him, but the woman to the right had been up with her baby and heard him come in but not go out again. She'd been awake until four a.m., her child unsettled and crabby. So if she was to be believed, Cribbins had told them the truth.

So why had he acted weird?

According to this bird, he'd been married once, but his wife had left him — he gambled — and it had torn their relationship apart. Bethany filed the info of him having an ex-wife away. It might come in handy later down the line. If she'd grown to hate him, she might be willing to tell them about his darker side, if he had one.

She drove to Jillbell Drive and left the car outside number nineteen. She needed a cup of coffee and hoped Noreen Withers would offer one. A wee wouldn't go amiss either. On the doorstep, she pressed the bell and waited, Mike standing behind her as the garden path was too narrow for them to present a united front, side by side.

A woman answered, in her seventies or eighties, with cotton-wool-white hair sitting in tonged curls on top of a head that was too big for her body. She was a wisp of a thing, four-foot-nothing in a tartan skirt, white blouse, and a grey homemade cardigan, chunky cable knit snaking up the fronts. American Tan tights concertinaed at her spindly ankles above maroon velour slippers.

Bethany let the lady study her ID while she explained who they were, then, "We'd like to follow up on the conversation you had with our colleague, Fran Davies, about Margaret and Harry Allthrop."

A smile. Dentures. "Yes, come along in. I've just boiled the kettle."

Thank God.

"And I've baked some biscuits. Shortbread, if you have a mind for a nibble."

Although she'd just eaten lunch, Bethany wasn't going to turn down a homemade biscuit or two, so she said they'd love that, then followed the old dear into a bright and airy kitchen, pretty modern. Noreen was a woman who obviously moved with the times. They settled at the table, and while Noreen made the drinks, she babbled about how cold the weather was for autumn, along with, "It wasn't like that in my day. Something's up with this planet, don't you think? The seasons are all screwed up."

Coffee and biscuits before them, Noreen sat and said, "Terrible to hear about Margaret going missing, then being found dead."

"Who told you?" Bethany asked. She took a bite of shortbread. Gorgeous.

"Well, Harry rang the other day — or it might be the other week; time means nothing to me. That's what getting old does. So, where was I? Oh yes, he rang to ask if I'd seen her. Margaret sometimes came here for a chat, see. Anyway," — she flapped a hand — "he said she'd gone missing, and it had been in the papers that she'd nipped to the Cotswolds, and I said that was weird, because she hadn't told me about that, and I'd only seen her the day before she was supposed to have left. The police lady on the phone let on that she was dead, and that upset me, you know, that Harry hadn't been the one to give me a ring."

"So you saw her *when*?"

"The day before she went missing. Don't ask when that was, because I won't know. But she was here, eating some coffee cake, remarking on how she'd missed it once I'd stopped working for her, and to be honest, I didn't have any sympathy for her regarding what she'd said. It's her fault she doesn't have my baking at her house anymore."

"Did you retire?"

"No, I haven't been there for many a long year. She said she didn't need any of us anymore once Harry had been taught how to do the jobs around the place. She had him learn from all of us since he was little, everything we knew, then when he was old enough — eighteen, it was — we got the sack, and he took our places. Charming, but it all worked out for the best in the end. Everyone was dying to leave anyway."

At last, a reason for someone to be disgruntled. "Was anyone upset about losing their jobs?" Bethany did the maths in her head. It had been a fair few years since Harry had been eighteen, a while to hold a grudge, but sometimes, people held things in for so long then snapped.

"We were all pleased, not upset. More of a relief, really, considering what Margaret was like."

"What *was* she like?"

"Oh, she was lovely in her own way at times but had a dark air about her that meant you didn't disobey. We were all a bit scared of her — she had a bark on her that was damn loud — and no one wanted to tell her they were unhappy working there in case she flipped her lid. Silly. We were all adults behaving like children, frightened of her the way we were. I look back on it now and wish I'd walked years ago, but there was Harry to think of. Leaving him in that setup when he was a minor wasn't something any of us wanted to do. We'd all grown fond of the lad and watched out for him as much as we could."

That was interesting. Margaret was all smiles and 'lovely' outside the house, but from what Noreen had said, she was different inside it.

"Fran told me you have something to tell us," Bethany said. "We'll listen to anything that might shed some light on why she was killed."

"She probably rubbed someone up the wrong way." Noreen nodded, sage as you like. "Margaret could be snippy, such an authoritarian, and it was all because of that rotten husband of hers. When I first started working there, Margaret was young and sweet. She had no idea what Elias was like — that's her husband, by the way. He was much older than her, and I think he wowed her with who he was — a distant cousin to an earl, so far removed they weren't acknowledged in the family. I suspect she imagined balls and flowing dresses, and there were a few that I recall, but the household was nothing like she thought it would be. She saw his fist more than a room full of party people and his boot in her stomach more than a shopping spree in Harrods."

"The reason she got involved with the refuge?"

"Yes. Once he died, she flung herself into it, using the money he'd left her to fund the very people he despised — women. He must have charmed her something chronic when he was dating her, then once they were married, the real him came out. Us staff knew what he was really like, and I tried to let Margaret know before the wedding, but she was having none of it. Of course she wouldn't, when all she saw was a nice kind man who'd do anything for her. But he was a bastard, plain and simple. Wolf in sheep's clothing, you know the sort."

"Why did she stay with him?"

"She told me once he put the fear of God into her. Said if she ever walked out, he'd find her, and the reason she kept Harry indoors all the time, not sending him out to school and such, is because Elias had said he'd kill the lad if he was ever out of her sight. He didn't like Harry because when he was born, Margaret devoted herself to him. Elias was a jealous man."

Christ, what a life.

"They only had the one child?" For all Bethany knew, poor Margaret could have miscarried because of a kick or punch to the abdomen.

"Yes. Margaret confessed to me once, after too much sherry, that Elias had told her sex was just for procreation, not for fun like she'd once thought."

Diana at the refuge said the same.

The old lady carried on. "Over the years, he'd convinced her so much about it that she told Harry the same thing. She was brainwashed. To be honest, Margaret was a different person altogether indoors. Nothing like the public woman she gave off. She came across as bitter and treated Harry like a slave. Her life hadn't turned out as she'd once hoped, and her son, who I have to say she'd adored once upon a time, became the focus of her hatred. If she was nice to Harry and Elias found out, she got beaten. Stands to reason that in her mind, if she put up a barrier between herself and her child, she wouldn't get hurt — and Harry wouldn't get killed by his bastard of a father. After Elias' death, Margaret continued that behaviour, but you'd think she'd have stopped it then."

"I'm struggling to comprehend this man, Elias. Was he seriously that much of a tyrant? Do you think he had it in him to kill his own son?"

Noreen nodded. "Definitely. He was another reason we dared not leave our jobs before he died. He said he'd make sure we never worked anywhere again, and we believed him. You have to understand the times we lived in. It's nothing like today, where you can speak to some ombudsman or other and fight your case. We didn't really have rights as such, and the ones that were in place, well, Elias ignored them. D'you know, I rather think Margaret took on his persona once he'd passed. She became the one thing she'd hated — a replica of him. Elias detested women, so she detested men. I actually think she lost the plot, and who could blame her? You had to live with them to realise what it was like. Me just telling you doesn't show the real horror."

"In the pictures I've seen of her online, she's all smiles and very kind." Bethany eyed Mike to see how he was taking this news. Margaret had clearly been an idol for him, yet he was finding out a very different story here.

He shrugged, maybe throwing off his previous perceptions and letting the new ones settle on his shoulders.

"Yes, she seemed to come alive outside those walls, allowing herself to be who she once was," Noreen said. "She was so cruel to Harry, though."

"Why didn't you tell anyone, the authorities, that Margaret was being abused and, in turn, she abused her son?" Mike asked her, his face skewed in annoyance.

"Would you tell the police if you thought your employer would hurt you or your family?" Noreen eyed him with a touch of disdain. "Like I said, you didn't know the times. You've been brought up knowing you can turn to anyone and help will be there. In my day, it was a far different matter. We were frightened, Elias saw to that, then Margaret took on his mantle, and that's why I still had her here for coffee from time to time. There was that fear inside me that if I didn't, something bad would happen. Still, I've told you now, it's out of me, so maybe I can rest easy."

Bethany took a sip or two of coffee to hide her feelings. A whole household of staff, scared to put a foot out of place. A woman, Margaret, forced to be someone she wasn't. And a son, that poor little boy, living an isolated life, his mother trying to protect him yet at the same time shunning him, hurting him.

"Do you know how Harry feels about all this?" Bethany took another biscuit. They really were the business.

"Well, he doesn't know any different, does he." Noreen broke a shortbread in half. "If that's all you know, you don't tend to question anything. There were no TVs in the house, you know, so that lad had no idea what the real world was like, other than hearing small snippets on my kitchen radio or when the staff were talking. I remember telling him stories, after he'd asked me to, and his eyes lit up in wonder, but there was also a smidgen of confusion. He was an adult then, so I didn't feel I was interfering with his upbringing. He'd come here to talk while his mother was at the refuge. She didn't like him leaving the house, even though he was a man, unless he was with her. I'd told him things he'd had no idea about, and he'd changed after that. I think he was about thirty at that point, and he'd just started venturing outside the house by himself."

"In what way did he change?"

"He got belligerent towards his mother, and quite right, too. He visited me again and said they'd had massive rows. He was cross she'd lied to him about the world, and she'd insisted he couldn't leave her, that he'd be killed if he did. So I had to explain that one to him and suggested that maybe Margaret's fear of her husband bumping off her son was so ingrained she'd forgotten he was dead and he couldn't do what he'd promised. Like I said, she went a bit mad."

Bethany put herself in Harry's shoes. Would she want to kill a mother who had secreted her away for years and, upon finding out she'd been told lies, would she lash out? Or was Stockholm Syndrome at play, and Harry still obeyed her no matter what, despite being 'belligerent'?

They'd definitely need to speak to him again, get him to open up, because if he *had* killed her, who knew who else he'd go after next if he felt others had played a part in his incarceration.

And let's face it, he was imprisoned.

She felt so sorry for him and almost couldn't blame him if he had murdered her.

She might well have done the same thing in his shoes.

CHAPTER SEVEN

Harry wasn't pleased. The police had been sniffing around, according to the man who'd dug the hole.

Harry had met him in a pub called The Lamb Shank, a rather strange name, but he'd learnt many a thing since he'd ventured out into the real world, and a lot of it showed life could be weird. The hole man, Aiden Parker, had answered the ad Harry had put in one of the little shop windows, which he'd paid for in cash and with a fake name: ODDJOB PERSON NEEDED. PLEASE CONTACT ME ON THIS NUMBER FOR DETAILS.

Aiden had called one of Harry's many cheap pay-as-you-go phones. Because Harry had certain things in mind, things he couldn't have traced back to him, he'd paid some kid to go in and buy a few, waiting in Mother's car, wondering if the boy would actually come back or leg it with the money.

Harry had told Aiden what he needed doing, saying he was a wildlife expert who wanted to catch a fox to study it. Aiden had said he didn't give a toss *what* Harry was, he'd get the borer, do the job, take the cash, and fuck off.

Harry had been withdrawing money from the family credit card for some time now. He was the accountant as well as the dogsbody, so Mother hadn't suspected a thing.

The phone call from Aiden this morning had disturbed Harry, and his plans had changed. Why were the police questioning the fellow who'd provided the borer, the one who worked at the wind place? What had he done to gain their attention? Did they know for sure it was him and were waiting for him to trip up?

That would lead to Aiden, then to Harry.

That couldn't happen.

Harry got on his father's old-fashioned motorbike, one that had been registered as scrap many moons ago. Harry had restored it over the years, creeping out into the garage while Mother wasn't around. A holdall on his back, he sped off to meet Aiden in one of the fields behind the house, one far enough away that it meant suspicion wouldn't fall on him. They were all bordered with high hedges, owned by a farmer three and a half miles away, so no one would see him doing what had to be done. While he travelled around the edges of the fields so he didn't leave tyre tracks in the crops, he thought about the letter he'd sent to the police regarding Selondra and surmised they were having trouble deciphering her last resting place like they had with Mother.

Thick bastards.

Ah, there was Aiden, who'd used a moped to get here. Harry had given him explicit instructions as to which route to take and not to come in a car, and he was pleased the man had done what he'd asked. Harry parked close to a hedge and got off, removing his helmet to place it on the grass. It was pointless hiding. He'd been stupid, naıve, when meeting Aiden last time. The man has seen his face.

Tugging his holdall off, he dumped it on the motorbike seat and opened it, sliding his hand inside and keeping it there. "You'll need to sort out that friend of yours who got the borer."

Aiden took his helmet off, too, and hung it on one of the moped handlebars. "I know."

"What's his name?"

"John Cribbins. He's going to get me right in the shit. His boss rang the police about the theft."

Lord Almighty, what the devil has been going on? "How did they even know it had gone? Didn't you take it back?" Harry's heart palpitated.

"I couldn't." Aiden had the grace to blush, but that wasn't going to solve anything, was it. The man had messed up.

"Why not?"

"I bloody fell asleep after I did the job for you."

"Excuse me? You went home afterwards? You didn't take the tool straight back?" Harry had a nasty feeling in his belly, a twisting knot of apprehension. "I paid you to jolly well return it."

"No, I didn't go home, and I *did* go to the wind place to return it, but it was four in the fucking morning, for God's sake, and I parked up. Only meant to shut my eyes for a minute or two, have a little kip, and the next thing I know, it's eight o'clock, and I didn't have time to put it back without being caught by staff arriving."

Oh God . . . "You do realise that if you'd done what I'd said, we wouldn't have a problem, don't you?" *You wouldn't have a problem, Aiden. A big one, coming your way very soon.*

Harry eyed Aiden in his black leather jacket with a collar that was buckled halfway up his neck — nowhere to stab his throat easily without hitting his jawbone if he didn't get it right. The weapon Harry had curled his hand around inside the holdall would be getting wet from his palm sweating if he didn't have gloves on. He had no choice but to do him in, especially with Aiden's confession.

"Where's the borer?" Harry demanded.

"I tipped it." Aiden gave an I-don't-give-a-shit shrug.

"Where?"

"Out in the sticks, down by a stream. I doubt any fucker will find it."

Harry had to hope some fucker *didn't* find it. Uneasy with this turn of events, he quickly assessed the distance between him and Aiden. The man was too far away for Harry to get a good strike, so he beckoned him closer with his free hand.

"Listen," Harry said. "We need to smooth this out, and I have a way to do it."

Aiden raised his eyebrows, clearly all ears.

"You see, it's like this . . ." Harry whipped the red-handled screwdriver out and plunged it into Aiden's eye.

Aiden screamed — good job they were in the middle of nowhere really — and crumpled down onto his knees, clutching his face, blood streaming between his fingers. Harry joined him down there, adrenaline thrumming through his veins, and rammed the screwdriver into Aiden's ear. The scream this time was that of an animal, wretched and beyond pain, so far removed from the usual that the agony must be infinite, pulsing on and on inside Aiden's head, piercing, so awful, so *there*. Aiden keeled over onto his side, revealing his throat the way his head tilted like that. Blood streaked the skin in rivulets, thick and oozing, and Harry yanked the screwdriver out and stabbed it in Aiden's ear again.

Again. Again. Again.

Aiden convulsed, his good eye bulging, a splatter of blood going right across his bright-blue iris. More blood, spurting out in fascinating, perfect arcs to drench the ground, seeping into it, nourishing the earth. Harry got up, moving away, conscious of getting too covered in claret. The smell of it was hideous, so much like the pennies he'd hoarded in his piggy bank as a child, given to him by Cook.

He stood and waited for Aiden to go still, then waited some more until the blood stopped streaking out, indicating the heart wasn't pumping. He stepped closer, felt Aiden's wrist for a pulse. Maybe the gloves were too thick, preventing him from picking up a faint flicker, but he was sure Aiden wouldn't come back from this.

With the screwdriver back in the holdall along with the eye, he took out a cheese grater. Standing on the other side of Aiden, where the ground was relatively free of red, he knelt and proceeded to file off Aiden's face skin, choosing the side of the grater that was used for lemon rinds and nutmeg. The side that hurt so much it was unreal. If Aiden had been alive, he'd have experienced the pain Harry had once felt when this very grater had sliced against his arse, Mother deciding that was a fitting punishment for what he'd done.

She'd been a wicked, evil bitch, and Harry was aware his mind was broken to be behaving this way but couldn't do a damn thing about it. He'd scraped the grater over *her* arse, too, before he'd dumped her in the hole, then a couple of days later, after she'd been incarcerated, kept away from humanity like he'd suffered for most of his life, he'd hauled her out and sliced off the skin, My Gorgeous pleased as punch that she'd exacted revenge. Then he'd taken the flesh home to dry it out and feed it to Selondra.

Bum jam.

He snapped himself out of the past and put the grater in his holdall. Helmet on, a smear of blood on the visor, he studied the area.

No farmer. No one at all.

Good.

He dumped the moped and helmet over the hedge into the adjacent field, got a number off Aiden's phone, then, climbing on Father's bike and revving the engine, he sped off for home, the place he detested yet loved at the same time. His prison had now become his sanctuary, where he'd lick his wounds after getting rid of all the people who had hurt him, then he'd live like he always should have, free of burdens, the king of his royal castle.

* * *

Harry had left the grain store outer door open, forgetting to lock it. Overnight, a family of field mice had got in and now ran rampant, dodging and weaving away from Cook's broom where she battled in vain to smack the buggers over the head before Mother found out what had happened.

"Shoo! Shoo!" she whisper-shouted, wielding her broom as though it were a sword. "If she finds out what young Harry did, we'll all be for it, every one of us."

Mother took misdemeanours out on everyone, seeing as the staff never admitted to who had done something wrong. They banded together, a tight-knit group who hated their employer but didn't have the guts to leave her.

Harry frowned. They were trapped just as much as he was, and when he grew up and became a man, he'd make sure Mother paid for how she treated everybody. Something deep inside told him it wasn't right, and knowing Cook and Milton the way he did, he knew they were good people and Mother wasn't.

Harry spent most of his life confused. Conflicting emotions warred within him on a daily basis, and he swung from adoring his mother to hating her, flummoxed at how he felt about it. She was his life, all he knew apart from the staff and the refuge ladies who visited once Father had died. Oh, and Tobias and Charles, who didn't come now after they'd introduced him to what boobies and minnies were.

"Good grief, where's that bleedin' cat when you need her?" Cook said, chasing the mice.

Harry pressed his back to the door that led to the kitchen, staring through the open doorway of the grain store, at the side garden where Milton had planted herbs, vegetables, and fruit. Runner bean stems had climbed up the bamboo sticks, bearing many long green beans, something Harry ate raw while Cook shelled peas out on the bench in the sunshine.

"I'll take the blame for this, never fear," Cook said to him. "If she sacks me, good. I could do with getting away from this place. It's cursed, I tell you."

Harry kept his mouth shut, wishing Cook would do the same. With all her roaring at the creatures, she'd be heard, and Mother would come along to see what the fuss was about.

"Got you!" Cook shrieked, a mouse unmoving beside her foot where she'd walloped it with the broom. "Now for the rest of you."

She smacked at them until one made a bid for freedom and disappeared into the side garden, the others following suit, a row of scampering little beasts chasing an unseen Pied Piper. Door slammed shut, Cook propped her broom next to it and dusted off her hands, same as she did when baking bread, except no flour puffed up into the air this time. She scooped up the dead mouse and threw it out into the garden.

"Into the kitchen now, and no one need be any the wiser," she said.

Harry turned the knob. Opened the door.

Mother stood there. "Any the wiser for what?" she said, hands on hips, her face a slice of stone.

Harry spun to gape at Cook, his legs going weak.

"Oh!" was all Cook managed, then she flushed bright red. "We had an accident. I spilt some flour from one of the sacks. All cleaned up now."

Mother barged past Harry and walked into the store, peering at the floor as though waiting to find a speck of flour. "That!" She pointed over by the sacks. "Is a mouse dropping."

Harry's stomach rolled over. "I was . . ."

Cook gave him a glare, sending him silent.

"You were what?" Mother asked. "Don't think about lying. If you do, I'll know."

He had to tell the truth. There was no point hiding it now. She'd get it out of him in the end anyway. Fear prodded him to speak. "I left the outer door open last night, and a load of mice came in."

Maybe someone else would get the blame. The doors were meant to be locked by an adult every evening before bed.

"Well . . ." Mother strode towards him. "Aren't you just a clever little dick?"

He didn't understand what she meant. How could it be clever to leave the door open when she'd always said it was forbidden? Confused, he blinked up at her.

"Go into The Study." She snarled it, nasty and raspy.

He ran, through Cook's kitchen and out into the foyer. Up the stairs, the Devil on his tail, and into The Study with its bare walls. As usual, he closed himself in and moved to the window, watching out for Milton, even though he wouldn't be there today. The gardener was off meeting his new fancy woman called Pam, who had short white hair like an old man and went on about things being 'the lawah'. Harry thought she meant 'law', but the way she said it was weird.

Sad that Milton wasn't there to give him a wave, instead taking Pam to some secret society place to do with Freemasons, whatever they were, dressing her as a man for some reason, Harry slumped to the floor and leaned on the wall. What was it like outside the grounds? What life existed? He knew some of it from listening to Cook and Milton talking, or other staff when they didn't know he was lurking. He tried to imagine what they'd described — lots of cars packing the streets, crowds of people, children playing in parks where they used things called swings and slides.

Someone was coming. Harry turned.

The door arced open, the handle cracking into the wall. Mother loomed there, seeming to fill the frame, and she held a cheese grater. Harry tried to figure out what she'd need it for.

"Pull your trousers down," she ordered.

Harry scrabbled to his feet and did as she'd asked, automatically showing her his back so she had better access to strike him. His pants were wrenched away from his bum, and something sharp in several places scraped his skin. It got harder and worse with every saw of it back and forth, and he cried out, begging her to stop.

But she didn't. She kept on, up and down, side to side, and something hot trickled down his leg. Blood? It had to be that, didn't it?

"If you ever lie to me again, I'll slice your backside off," she said.

The door snicked shut. Harry swivelled to make sure she'd really gone, sobs wrenching out of him, chest juddering.

Years later, once he realised Mother had lied to him, *he'd vowed, when the time was right, that he'd slice* her *backside off. After all, it was her own threat of punishment for him, so she should be willing to take a spoonful of her own medicine.*

* * *

Harry scrubbed the screwdriver and grater and placed them in a clean holdall. My Gorgeous glinted at him from the draining board as if telling him off for not using her. Her anger was as sharp as her blade. He sensed it keenly.

"You only come out to play for the other people," he told her, hoping she didn't pick up on his voice shaking. "Aiden was an extra, as is John Cribbins." He walked through into what used to be the grain store but was now a utility room. He stuffed his dirty holdall into the washing machine on a ninety-degree cycle, then went back to collect his second one, slung it on his back and strutted outside to climb on the motorbike. Cribbins would be meeting him shortly at the fifth turbine, far enough away from Shadwell Wind Energy not to attract attention. Far enough away that Cribbins' screams wouldn't be heard.

He drove off, whistling, wondering when Selondra would be found.

CHAPTER EIGHT

John was still shaking after receiving the phone call from that bloke who'd asked Aiden to steal the borer. He'd called himself The Avenger, and John had wondered whether he watched too many films. The Avenger wanted to meet, but John, uneasy, hadn't wanted to. Trouble was, the lure of more money had been strong and sealed the deal, and, as luck would have it, Yentis had come along and asked John to do the daily turbine inspection for him. Something about Yentis' kid needing to be picked up from school a bit earlier than usual. John didn't give a shit *what* Yentis had to do, only that John had the perfect opportunity to do what The Avenger had asked.

John left the building, twirling the company Jeep keys, getting in and starting the engine. He had a few minutes before he had to meet The Avenger at turbine five, so he reckoned he'd look at the others on his way up there, studying the arms for any bird debris, namely bodies, where the stupid prats had flown into them and ended up being dead for their trouble.

What did The Avenger want, though? He hadn't said, just mentioned he'd got John's number off Aiden's phone and he needed John to help him with another job — putting the borer back. John couldn't snip the security camera wires, not again. He'd said so, and that had been when five hundred quid had been dangled, and he'd fallen for it. He could pay next month's mortgage with that and get ahead of the game for once instead of lagging behind.

There had to be some other way of doing things without the CCTV being involved, and that was what John was going to suggest to The Avenger. They could reach some agreement, then everything would go back to normal.

With the first four turbines visually inspected, he drove on towards the fifth, which was farther along, about a quarter of a mile. There had been others filling the gap in the past, but they'd suffered a lightning strike and had been taken down. Vellord kept going on about replacing them but hadn't got around to it.

In the distance, someone stood beside a motorbike, and John slowed, his subconscious at work most likely, stalling the inevitable. How could that borer be put back without John having to do anything that could get him in the shit? Ah, he'd tell The Avenger to get Aiden to just drop it off at the main gates in the dead of night. Those new security fellas would spot it eventually. Yep, that was a good plan.

He arrived and cut the engine, then got out. The Avenger still had his helmet on, and John idly wondered where the fella's cape was and had to hold back a giggle. Then he had the sense that something was off. He ought to get in the Jeep really, go back to work, forget about the money, and leave The Avenger to sort things on his own.

An open holdall sat on the bike seat.

Does it have his mask in it? His shield? No, don't crack up laughing now.

John stopped in front of the bloke, coaching himself to behave. "Listen, I had this really good idea—"

A screwdriver came towards him in the biker's fist. The tip plunged into his eye, and the pain was unlike anything he'd ever known. His bowels opened, and wet, hot heat seared his arse. Agony raged through his head, and his brain seemed to short out.

"You silly, silly boy," The Avenger said. "I shall have to grate your face now."

Grate my face?

John couldn't see out of his other eye either. Tears blurred his vision, and torture speared his brain. He blinked, seeing again now, and lifted a hand to pull out the screwdriver, but The Avenger got there first, yanking it away. John crashed to the ground and, despite the horrendous pain and his good eye misting again, he stared at his other eye skewered on the end of the screwdriver.

"I wonder what my next dinner guest will make of your flesh?" The Avenger said, advancing towards John, a cheese grater in hand.

John's bladder gave up the fight and released all the urine he'd been holding in since this morning. Then . . . hello, grater, meet face.

CHAPTER NINE

Bethany and Mike arrived in the incident room, and Bethany related what she'd found out from Noreen Withers, then added it to the whiteboard. Fran and Leona had managed well without having to call anyone else in for help, and all lines of enquiry were almost up to date. Friends had been spoken to, but John Cribbins' ex-wife hadn't — Fran had been about to do that when Bethany and Mike had turned up.

"Okay, give her a bell now," Bethany said. "I need the loo. Won't be a tick."

She had her toilet break then returned to the others. Fran was still on the phone, her eyebrows high, and she waved Bethany over.

"I think you need to speak to my DI," Fran said.

Bethany took the phone. "Gina Cribbins? I'm DI Bethany Smith."

"I'm not Cribbins anymore, I changed back to my maiden name. It's Fields now. I was just telling Mrs Davies about the van she mentioned."

Bethany went cold, and adrenaline flounced around inside her, a dancer on foxtrot toes. "What van?" She'd probably sounded desperate, but to be fair, she bloody was.

"My ex has this well annoying mate called Aiden, and John used to borrow the Transit from time to time. It's a white one."

"Aiden who?" Bethany grabbed a pen out of Fran's mug that had a cartoon picture of a uniformed copper on the side.

"Parker. He's a bit of a knob, to be honest, and part of the reason me and John split up. Apart from the gambling, that is."

"I see." Bethany scribbled the name down and gestured for Fran to get cracking on finding his address. "What's Mr Parker like?"

"A bloody thief and the sort who'd even rob a granny if he could get away with it. A right old piece of work, although he isn't violent or anything, just a prat."

Fran tapped her screen to get Bethany's attention. An address and photograph greeted her of a bald man who resembled Ross Kemp doing one of his documentaries. Parker's current job was down as a car dealer, his previous a joiner, a barman, and a stripogram.

Oo-bloody-er.

He had a few priors, but nothing major: a fight in a pub, driving while under the influence, and a row in the street with the neighbours, which had resulted in him flinging a spanner at someone and bruising the man's eye.

"Where does he live, do you know?" Bethany focused on her feet and waited to see if the addresses matched.

"Last I heard, he was still living on Shadwell Heights. John lives there, too, in our old place. Sorry, I don't know Aiden's exact address. I wasn't interested in getting to know the likes of him when I was married to John."

"Doesn't matter. How do you get on with John now?"

"I prefer to keep my distance."

"Strange question, but do you know if Mr Parker owns a generator?"

"As a matter of fact, I do. John used it once for my niece's bouncy castle. The damn thing was well loud. Felt like we were at the fair."

Bethany wanted to laugh with relief that they had a line they could follow. "Okay, thanks. Is there anything else you can think of that we might need to know about Mr Parker and John?"

"Only that I heard him and John are thick as thieves now, more than ever, which is amusing, considering that's what they are. Someone told me John had been helping Aiden nick stuff recently. I'd say I'm surprised, but John took one of my rings to sell once to feed his gambling addiction, and that's why I don't mind grassing him up to you."

Bethany's heart clattered. "What sort of stuff are they stealing?"

"Machinery. Don't know what."

Yes! "Where did you hear that?"

"In the supermarket, of all places. I bumped into an old neighbour who works at the Shank. She heard the pair of them gassing about it while they were pissed out of their heads, the stupid dicks. I mean, who talks loudly about those types of jobs? Anyway, I hope you catch them. It's disgusting that they think they can just go around pinching things."

"Thank you very much, Gina, you've been really helpful. Are you willing to give me the name of the lady who told you this?"

"I don't want her knowing it was me."

"I won't be telling her that. What I'll do is go there to question the Shank staff about thefts and see if she says anything, then steer the conversation in the right direction."

"Her name's Rita. You can't miss her. Bottle blonde, she is, with bright-pink eyeshadow. I don't know her surname."

"Thanks again." Bethany handed the phone back to Fran for her to wind up the conversation.

Writing down Aiden Parker's address, she then ripped the sheet of paper from the Post-it pad and walked over to Mike at his desk.

"We're off again," she said. "Looks like we have a lead on who might have stolen the borer. Can you do a quick search on this bloke's vehicles." She stuck the note to the top corner of his monitor so he could input the info into the computer.

It brought up several cars, a moped, and the Transit, which was there in all its nineteen-nineties reg glory.

"Come on then." She led the way to the door, telling Fran and Leona where they were going.

The journey didn't take long, and she shook off the unease at having to be on this bloody estate again. First, they stopped off at the Shank, and thankfully, Rita was working. She said she'd gladly tell all about the conversation between Cribbins and Parker.

"Well," she said, holding her boobs up with her folded arms, "it goes like this. They were propping up the bar, John more than half cut after sponging drinks off Aiden because he'd once again lost his money in that fruit machine over there. He might as well be married to the fucking thing these days. Anyway, Aiden mentioned five hundred quid, so of course, the old ears perked up, didn't they. I loaded the glass washer, which is right by where they were standing, and made out I wasn't listening. The five hundred was for John to turn off the cameras at the wind place and make sure some tool or other was put by the door."

"Did he mention what the tool was?"

Rita nodded. "Something to do with cutting great big holes in the bloody ground. John must have been as interested as me, because he asked why Aiden would want to cut a hole. So Aiden says, 'Some wildlife bloke needs to catch a fox.' I thought that was a bit weird, but oh well, not my business. So John agreed to do what Aiden wanted, and John asked how much Aiden was getting for his side of the job. Aiden told him to piss off and mind his own business, then they got to bickering, which was boring, and I had to serve a customer then."

Bethany's heartbeat livened up at that. "Can you remember when this conversation was?"

Rita gazed at the ceiling, then back at Bethany. "Got to have been about two weeks ago. Oh yeah, just remembered.

The bloke who wanted the hole dug, the fox fella, he was going to pay Aiden beforehand, and Aiden said he'd considered running off with the cash and not doing the work, but he decided against it because Foxy was weird and it might turn to shit on him."

"Did he elaborate on that?"

"Not really, just that he spoke funny, and that could be anyone, couldn't it." Rita smiled.

"Thanks very much for all that. We'll be in touch if we need to speak to you again."

"No problem," Rita said. "Those two need pulling up and stopping. They're known for pinching bits and bobs, and I told Gina, John's ex, that he was getting himself into all sorts lately, more than the small things he used to do when they were married. Mind you, she didn't know about that at the time. It was only after they split that people told her."

Bethany said goodbye, and they ended up at Parker's address, an old-fashioned terrace with cream pebbledash on the outer walls. All the vehicles he owned apart from the moped lined the kerb outside the property and beyond. The Transit sat a few doors down. If he was a car dealer, he might well be running his business from home.

They walked up the path, and Bethany knocked on the door. After a couple more raps with no answer, she led the way back down the path. At the gate, she paused at someone opening up next door.

"He's not in," a ragged young woman said, black hair all over the shop, Medusa on steroids. "Went out on that bloody moped of his, the noisy fucker. I tell you, he revs it up until you can't hear yourself think, and all this smoke comes out of the exhaust, which isn't good for my asthma."

Bethany introduced them and walked to the woman's front door. "Do you know him well?"

"Ooh, you're coppers. Well, can you do something about his vehicles because the council haven't bothered? He takes up all our parking spaces with them. And as for that moped smoke, that's emissions, that is, so you ought to sort that an' all. And no, I don't know him well. He's lived here for about five years but only speaks to people to give them a mouthful, and as for that bleedin' genny of his, well, there's been plenty of times I've wanted to knock his block off because he fires it up in the back of his van." She pointed to the Transit.

"So you wouldn't have any idea where he might have gone earlier?" Bethany asked.

"Nope, and I don't want to. He's a bad lot, that's what I think."

"Does he speak to anyone down here or does he keep to himself?"

"Try that git on the other side of him. He's always out here working on the cars."

"What's the git's name?" Bethany grinned.

The woman returned it. "Paul something or other. I only know that because Aiden shouts at him, and I only know Aiden's called Aiden because Paul shouts back."

Mike cleared his throat, a signal that he had the need to laugh. Bethany wound the conversation up, and they strode away.

"My God, is she all there up top?" Mike asked.

"I don't know, but she told us a few things, so she's all right in my book."

They went to the Transit and peered through the back windows. A generator sat inside.

"That's what I wanted to see," she said. "Now let's check if The Git is in."

Mike laughed and knocked on Paul's door. It swung open, and a weedy, brown-haired man who appeared to need food in his belly stood there, ribs prominent beneath his bared chest, reminiscent of open Venetian blinds.

"What do you fucking want?" he asked, his eyes piggy as though they'd roused him from a deep sleep.

"Paul, is it?" Bethany held up her ID.

"If you're here because that prick sold the dodgy Vectra, that's nothing to do with me. I told him that engine wasn't right, but would he listen? Would he 'eck."

"We're not here about the Vectra," she said. God, it was hard not to giggle. Some days, the people they spoke to poked her funny bone. "Do you know where Mr Parker is?"

"Pissed off out on the moped," he said. "Without giving me my wages, so I'm dogged off with him."

"Do you know where he might have gone?"

Paul scratched his spindly nose. "Yeah, he was meeting some bloke in a field, the same bloke he'd done a job for recently. And if you're also here about that sodding borer, that was nothing to do with me. He asked me to help him dump it, and I told him to get on his bike." He chuckled. "Did you see that, what I just did? On his bike . . . and he *is* on his bike . . ."

Mike gave a titter that said he couldn't believe they'd spoken to two people who seemed a bit off their rockers. "Funny."

"I thought so," Paul said. "Anyway, he fly-tipped the bugger down by that massive oak next to the stream. Towland Road, know where I mean?"

Bethany nodded. "Thank you."

"And you can tell him it was me who got him in the shit an' all." Paul jabbed at the air. "He owes me money, and I don't take kindly to that. I'll bloody kill him when I next see him."

"I wouldn't advise that," Mike said and gave him a stern look. "Besides, if you did that, he can't pay you, can he. Then we'll be back here, asking all sorts, like what you were up to at the time Mr Parker was killed."

"I didn't mean it like that!" Paul's ribs quivered in his indignation. "What I meant was . . ."

They walked away, leaving Paul scowling.

"You cheeky bleeders," Paul shouted. "You can't just walk off like that when I'm speaking!" The sound of the door slamming was loud behind them.

In the car, they almost wet themselves, tears streaming down Bethany's face. God, she hadn't laughed like this in ages, and it felt good to have her stomach hurting and her jaw aching from it.

"Fuck me," Mike managed. "We're apparently cheeky bleeders. These people are sent to try us, I reckon."

She wiped her face. "We need to sober up before we get to the next stop." She gunned the engine. "Ring Rob for me and tell him about the borer and have someone go down there and see if it's by the oak. If it is, it'll need to go to forensics."

Mike spoke to Rob while Bethany drove, and she headed towards Shadwell Wind Energy. John Cribbins had some bloody explaining to do. Once there, she parked, and they went inside, receiving a pleased smile from Lisa.

"Is John Cribbins in?" Bethany asked.

"Yes, hang on a second." Lisa picked up her desk phone and pressed a button. "Mr Vellord, is John at his computer? He went out to do the turbines instead of Yentis, and I haven't seen him come back in." She cringed and stood, then walked around the desk to the glass front doors, cordless phone pressed to her ear. "Because Yentis had to go and pick up his daughter early. She's ill." A few blinks, then, "No, the Jeep isn't there, but the other one is." A heartbeat. "It's just that the police are here to speak to him again." A pause. "Okay." She walked back and replaced the receiver. "John hasn't returned from a job, but Mr Vellord will come out and talk to you now."

Bethany thanked her. Had John done a runner, stealing the Jeep?

Vellord barged out into reception, face ruddy, eyes bulging. "I swear to God, that man . . ." He approached and shook their hands. "Come this way." He guided them to a small office and closed the door. "Can I help you instead of John?"

"I'm afraid John might have been involved in the borer theft," Bethany said and went on to fill him in with the details, including who had used the tool.

"Aiden bloody Parker! He worked here, and I caught him being a bully to one of the school children who'd come for a tour, and that was the last straw. He was sacked. I should have known this was something to do with him." He sighed.

"Give me two seconds while I see where John is. I had no idea he'd gone to the turbines instead of Yentis." He pulled a pair of binoculars out of his desk and peered through them out of the window. "Well, it looks like a vehicle is at turbine five. Shall we go along there and see what's going on?" He put the binoculars on the desk.

Bethany nodded, and they trooped out of the building, got into another Jeep, and made the first part of the journey in silence.

Then Vellord piped up. "We have to inspect them daily because of the dopey birds." He looked at them in the rear-view. "They smack into the rotor arms, see. If they do that where the rotors are attached, their guts and feathers can muck things up, the gears and whatever."

Nerves crowded Bethany's belly, and it wasn't to do with bird guts. Something was wrong. "What time would John have gone out there?"

"About an hour or so ago. Put it this way, if he's fallen asleep in that Jeep — Oh shit!"

Bethany jerked forward to peer between the seats.

Fuck.

John hadn't fallen asleep, or if he had, someone or something had taken chunks of his face off first. And removed his eye.

Mike shot out of the vehicle, saying, "Stay put. I'll go." He rushed towards John, pulled a glove out of his pocket, put it on, then felt for a pulse at his neck. He shook his head and stepped back, then returned to the Jeep.

He rang Rob to call it in. It only took five minutes for a uniform to arrive and stand guard by the body.

"Take us back to the centre, please," Mike said to Vellord.

Vellord let out a stream of cursing and reversed, then did a three-point turn and sped back towards the building. "What the fucking hell? Oh my God. Bloody shit!"

Bethany watched him in the rearview. He was bricking it, his reaction one of genuine terror at having come upon a dead employee.

"I know it's hard, but try to remain calm," she told him. "Take a deep breath." Her heart thundered, so God knew what his was doing. She listened to Mike calling Isabelle next, and once Vellord had parked up, she left Mike to it, taking Vellord back inside towards the small office.

"Everything all right?" Lisa asked.

"I'm afraid not," Vellord said.

"We'll discuss that soon," Bethany butted in. She didn't need him blurting out that John was dead. Not just yet. Ushering Vellord into the office, she said, "I just need to talk to my colleague a second." She pointed to the coffeemaker. "Pour yourself a drink, and please, don't ring or talk to anyone about this for the moment. It's very important that you don't. I'll explain why in a bit."

She stepped into reception, and Mike stood outside, still on the phone. She went to him, and after he'd ended the call, she said, "More uniforms on the way as well?"

"Yes." He nodded. "The staff will have to be spoken to, and we'll need to be by the body so can't be the ones to do it."

"I agree. I'll just nip back in to see Vellord." She entered the building and found him pacing in front of the reception desk, coffee in hand. To Lisa, she said, "Did Yentis come back?"

Lisa nodded.

She'd get uniforms to talk to him. He could be the bloody killer.

"Can we just talk over here a minute?" she asked Vellord and gestured to the main doors.

They strode across.

"I'm going to need your help," she said quietly. "No employee can leave the premises at the moment, and I want you to make sure they don't. Uniforms will be arriving soon, and they'll deal with speaking to your staff because myself and Mike need to be with John." She glanced at Lisa to let Vellord know she didn't want to mention the death to her yet. She lowered her voice even more. "Don't tell anyone what's happened. We need everyone's genuine reaction, understand? If they're forewarned, they have a chance to school their features."

"Who would do such a wicked thing?" he whispered, hand shaking, coffee sloshing over the rim of his cup.

"I know it's difficult, and you've had a terrible shock, but please, we need you to do this."

He straightened his shoulders, self-importance giving them a solid edge, and nodded.

"Ah, here they are." She pointed outside.

Tory Yates and Nicola Eccles spoke to Mike while the SOCO van stopped and Isabelle poked her head out. Mike pointed to where John's body was, and the van trundled in that direction. Tory and Nicola came in, and Bethany gave them instructions, specifically about Yentis, leaving Vellord in their capable hands.

A message came through from Isabelle — seeing Bethany must have jogged her memory. Bethany read it, shocked and a tad disturbed, and, since she couldn't be in two places at once, she'd have to delegate. She rang Fran to ask her and Leona to do her a favour. After that, she went outside to get in her car with Mike and see up close the mess John Cribbins had been reduced to.

CHAPTER TEN

Milton and Pam sat at the kitchen table with Cook. Harry came closer, hoping they'd ask him to take a pew and join them for a cup of tea. Mother had gone out somewhere and had told him to behave himself while she was gone. He'd played for a bit in the nursery but had got bored.

"Ah, it's Harry," Milton said. "Come and have a bit of this cake here." He pointed at a large strawberry gateau, one Harry had helped Cook bake and ice this morning.

Harry sat, and Cook got up to get him a can of Coke from the walk-in fridge.

She plonked it on the table. "As usual, don't you be letting on you had that."

Harry smiled. Cook shared her Cokes with him sometimes, and those were the best days, because it meant Mother wasn't home. He pulled the tab and drank some, shivering at the bubbly burn on his tongue and throat.

Cook sat. "Carry on then, Pam."

"Well," Pam said, stirring her tea. "I told the man we couldn't possibly do what he wanted because it's against the lawah."

Harry dipped his head as Milton passed him a slice of cake, and he busied himself eating it. He loved listening to their tales. It gave him hope that one day he might leave this house and do so many things, just like they did.

"What did he want you to do?" Cook asked.

"Have some money put in my account, then I was to send it to him." Pam sluiced her teeth with her tongue, cleaning off the cake. "But like I said, the money was from a scam, and I could get in trouble for it."

"What did he say to that?" Cook asked.

Milton slapped the table.

Harry jumped, fearful of such noises.

Milton roared, "He said she was a bitch." He blushed. "You didn't hear me say that, lad."

Harry smiled and continued eating, his heart rate calming now he knew it was only Milton who'd created the racket.

"That's awful," Cook said.

"Oh, I know." Pam stuffed more cake in her mouth.

"Would you like to come and pick some strawberries?" Cook asked Harry.

He nodded.

"Eat up, then we'll go out. Your mother wants them for the refuge lunch tomorrow. They're having a picnic on the grounds." She turned to Pam. "It must be awful for those poor women and children."

Harry tuned them out. It hadn't been so long ago that he'd watched his father hurt his mother. Even though a few years had passed, it was still fresh in his mind. Why hadn't Mother taken them to the refuge? Why couldn't they have been safe, eating strawberries with no worries?

She'd be home soon.

As though the thought of her made that so, Mother thundered into the kitchen, in a flurry and swish of her flowery summer dress, straw hat on at a tilt, her face wreathed in a smile. It was short-lived, though. She spotted the Coke in front of Harry and stomped across the room to snatch it away.

"Who said you could have this?" She glared down at him, cheeks going pink.

"It was me." Cook stood, stretching her frame to its full height. Although smaller than Mother, she exuded authority, despite confessing once that she was scared of her. "I thought the lad could have a treat. He has little to look forward to in this house."

Harry frowned. This didn't make sense. Cook had never stood up to Mother before. Perhaps it was because Pam was here. Usually, Mother ruled the roost and the staff cringed.

"That's none of your concern," Mother said. "Get up and come with me." She glowered at Harry.

He rose, upset that he wouldn't be able to pick the strawberries now and listen to Cook's stories. Mother left the room, and he followed, quick to keep up with her in case she turned round and he was too far behind. She took him into The Study, where she flayed his arse with one of Father's belts, railing at him about being a vile little man and if he continued in this way, she'd have to kill him.

No, that wouldn't be happening. Not if he killed her first.

* * *

With the grater and screwdriver scrubbed and now soaking in the washing-up bowl with bleach, Harry threw the memories into the back of his head and instead entertained images of those detectives being called out to view Cribbins' body. The man's eye, along with Aiden's, Mother's, and Selondra's, currently sat in a jar of vinegar, beside My Gorgeous, who winked at him, no doubt wishing she could slice them all in half.

Those detectives were going to get quite the shock, but that was their problem. They'd signed up for the job, so they shouldn't moan when something more . . . murderously explicit came their way.

What was it Cribbins had said just before the grating had become too much? "Tell Gina I love her."

That had set Harry off, singing away, replacing Gina for Laura, and the old sixties tune had seen him through the rest of the killing. Music was good for things like that, and he'd stabbed the screwdriver into Cribbins' ear and temple to the beat of the song. It was nice to know things the police didn't. It gave him the upper hand, so to speak. An edge. Something he hadn't had before Mother had died.

Was she on a slab now, being dissected?

He hoped so. And later, she'd be stored in the fridge while the investigation continued.

And she deserved to be there, the hateful bitch.

He scrutinised the walk-in fridge he'd been put in as a child and shuddered.

Life was so very cruel, wasn't it?

* * *

Selondra didn't move. He'd finished doing the procreation dance and stared down at her, wondering why she appeared so angry.

"Is that it?" she said, glaring up at him, a hint of malice in her eyes. "Is that all I get?"

"That's all you're meant to get, isn't it?"

She laughed then, long and loud and irritating, and pushed him off her — hard. He rolled onto the bed beside her, flat on his back, the ceiling with its rose around the light flex mocking him. The pattern of petals on it seemed to wave at him, broadcasting his incompetence, his inability to know what to do with almost everything.

"No." She stood to collect her discarded clothing. "You're meant to take care of your woman first. Pleasure her. You don't even know how to have sex properly."

"Pardon?" He frowned, not understanding at all. "What sort of pleasure?"

And she'd gone on to tell him, in massive detail, all he'd done wrong and all he could do right in the future. Anger burned inside him, and a scarlet mist descended.

Red is the colour of a man scorned.

Mother had lied. She'd punished him in the past for doing that very thing, yet she'd been spouting rubbish all along.

"Are you telling me you honestly have no idea what you're doing?" Selondra shimmied into her black sequin dress.

That mocked him as well, the way it glinted in the lamplight, the fucking bastard thing.

"Try porn," she said. "Surely you know what that is."

No, he didn't.

"Tell me," he said.

She laughed again then explained, and he cringed at the thought of watching people touching willies, boobies, and minnies. It didn't gel with what he'd been told by Mother, yet surely Selondra wouldn't make this up. The idea that people sucked nipples, though . . . No, too disturbing altogether.

He had some learning to do, but would Mother's tales prevent him from doing so? Would he fight against trying new things because she'd told him they were bad?

From time to time, she'd mumbled that he couldn't go out of her sight because someone would kill him. He'd often wondered if she'd gone mad at some point and told him nonsense so he'd be frightened and stay with her.

And it had worked.

"Better yet," Selondra said. "Go to Ann Summers and buy a few things."

Who was she? Some woman who sold rude items?

So Selondra didn't think him a complete imbecile, he didn't answer about Ann and instead said, "I don't think that's for me, the watching thing." Suddenly self-conscious, he dragged the quilt over his withering manhood. "I don't think any of it is."

"Well now, let's see." Selondra slid her knickers on then pulled a stocking up her thin, pasty-white leg. "If you want to see me again, you'd better take a crash course in sex. I can't even begin to imagine the percentage of people who only do it for procreation, but you can bet it's very low. What on earth have you been doing all your life?" The second stocking followed, creating the illusion her legs were tanned.

Harry wanted to rip them off and stuff them in her mouth so she couldn't breathe. She'd thrown his mind into confusion, and now he'd question everything Mother had ever told him. His world was quickly spinning out of control, and he sensed a panic attack coming on.

"Get out," he said. "Go on, piddle off."

She grabbed her clutch bag that matched her cerise high-heeled shoes and stood at the end of the bed, that bloody dress of hers still winking at him. "So, you expect me to shag then shoot, is that it?"

"I have no idea what you mean."

"No, seems you don't know a lot at all — about many things. And there was your mother, telling me you were a catch and someone I ought to set my sights on. You know what, Harry? You're quite useless to me. All these dates you've taken me on, acting like a complete fool in the restaurants, as though you don't even know how to behave in them

— I mean, who doesn't give tips? — then the walks by the river, which, I suspect, were meant to be romantic, but instead, I tromped in fucking horse manure or whatever it was . . . Really! A catch? Not bloody likely. I'll be telling your mother we're not ever going to be an item and to find you someone else. Someone who doesn't mind a quick poke in bed that does absolutely nothing for her."

She flounced out. Thank goodness Mother wasn't in so she wouldn't know they'd rowed. Shame burned Harry, his face heating, his head spinning. Selondra had said some cruel things, but a lot of it rang true. How could he face her again after this? She'd be at the refuge, and Mother wouldn't hear of him not going there to help her. She'd dock his wages.

He'd have to get rid of Mother for lying and Selondra for telling the truth.

There was no other way to move forward.

He closed his eyes and thought about the other two people who'd hurt him as much as those two bitches had. They'd all have to go to. Only then could he move on with his life.

Only then could he be free.

* * *

The doorbell rang, wrenching him out of the past. Who could that be? He stared at his tools in the bowl, then at My Gorgeous. She frowned at him, and her voice floated in his head: *Don't answer it. Don't let them in.*

He had to, though. Whoever it was needed to see him acting perfectly normal, not as a killer with four bodies on his list so far, two more than he'd intended, but that couldn't be helped. As Cook was fond of saying: *What's done is done.*

Wasn't that the truth.

He shoved the grater, screwdriver, and My Gorgeous in the dishwasher — she still had some of Selondra's blood on her handle — tossed in a tablet, then set the machine on its cycle. The eyes in the jar glared at him, irises surrounded by burst white matter, bloodied where he'd stabbed them to the side, so he threw a black-and-white-striped tea towel over the jar and set off for the front door, whistling for effect.

Two women stood on the step, blonde, in their late thirties if he was any judge. What, were they going to spout God at him? Neither of them held a pamphlet, so perhaps that wasn't their reason for being here at all.

"Yes?" he said, giving them his best smile, the one that hid all the tears and sadness, the evil and the lies.

One of them held up some ID.

Had they come for him?

Please, not yet. Not until I've got rid of the others. And even then, don't come for me.

I just want a proper life.

"I'm DC Fran Davies, and this is DC Leona Clinton. We need to ask a few questions on behalf of our DI, Bethany Smith."

"Ah, yes. Do come in. Would you like a coffee or tea?"

They exchanged glances. Leona shrugged, and Fran smiled at her, as though the idea of a drink while on duty was naughty.

"That would be nice." Fran walked in, smelling the same as Milton's roses.

Leona followed, and Harry closed the door then led them to the kitchen. My Gorgeous growled inside the dishwasher, disliking the women immediately, and the eyes yelled out for help, the words garbled from the vinegar, muffled by the jar.

"Hush now, you noisy buggers," Harry said.

"What was that?" Fran asked, raising her eyebrows.

"Oh, my stomach. It grumbled, so I told it off." He laughed, hoping it sounded genuine and not the false babble he'd heard it as.

"We know the feeling." Leona took a seat at the table. "Some days, it's like our throat's been cut."

A quick flash of Mother's arse cheek being sliced off zipped through his mind. Selondra's neck . . . He blinked and harrumphed.

"Oh, so sorry. I have no manners. Yes, do sit down." He poured coffee from the carafe while Fran popped herself next to her colleague, and after he'd been informed of sugar and cream, yes for both, he carried their drinks over.

"Oh, these cups and saucers are dead posh," Fran said. "I'll be worried about dropping them."

"I wouldn't care if you did." He'd given them Mother's best china, the set with hand-painted flowers she'd never used because it cost so much. Really, he ought to smash the bloody lot just to spite her ghost. "They're not my thing. Actually, you can have them if you want."

"Uh, no, but thank you," Fran said. "We're not allowed to do that. You could perhaps sell them at auction? I'd say they're worth a bob or two."

She smiled, and he decided he liked her. Also, it didn't seem they were here to arrest him. They were too casual, too kind for that rum business.

"How can I help you?" He sat with them, his coffee in his old *Thomas the Tank Engine* mug. Mother had bought it for him in his twenties.

"Oh, love your cup. My daughter likes Thomas," Fran said. "Okay, let's get to it. We just need to ask you a couple of things about your mother. I'm so sorry if it's distressing. We're aware of how raw things are."

Not as raw as Parker's and Cribbins' faces. Ha ha!

"No, that's absolutely fine," he said.

"We picked her car up from the garage, and forensics have found a few things we needed clarifying."

"Okay . . ." What could this be about? He'd only driven the damn thing for authentic reasons. He'd used Father's old jalopy with the sidecar attached to ferry Mother to the hole and Selondra to — "What's that then? The clarification, I mean."

"Well, a couple of things were found that may well cause you embarrassment, so please forgive me for asking, but would your mother have had sex toys and certain magazines in her vehicle?"

"Sex toys?" he blustered, heart ticking wildly. "Most certainly not! What were they like?"

Fran blushed and sipped her tea.

Leona took over. "A plastic vagina and magazines showing sex acts."

Well, she didn't beat around the bush.

Harry's guts travelled south with a mind to stay there. He came over all squiffy. Mother had found his things. She must have taken them out of his room and planned to dispose of them. Why hadn't she done that before leaving the car at the garage, the silly woman?

"They were in a locked box," Leona said, "which had to be forced open."

Ah, his box. Mother had most probably found the key for it to know what was inside.

Should he admit to it all being his? He'd only bought them in that Ann Summers shop — thank goodness, a shop, not a woman — in order to learn more about *things* after entertaining Selondra, and look where it had got him: in a cripplingly awful situation with members of the law.

Lawah.

He almost giggled.

Instead, he cleared his throat. "I'm afraid they're mine." They would only find out later down the line, so there was no point in lying. "You can dispose of them. I . . . uh . . . didn't use them, if you see what I mean."

"No, we realise that — the, um, the toy was still in the plastic packet," Leona said.

The pair of them had red cheeks, and Harry's burned — more from anger that Mother had been poking about in his room and had discovered them. He should have known privacy wasn't something she'd afford him, even though he was an adult.

"I'm terribly sorry you had to come here about this," he said. "I have no idea why she'd have my things. Perhaps she wanted to get rid of them." *No perhaps about it.*

"It's okay, it's all part of our job." Fran smiled. "What's your life like?"

He hadn't expected that, straight off the back of talking about the rude items. "What do you mean?"

"We have information that suggests you might be a loner, someone who doesn't venture out of the home a lot."

So someone had been talking. Who could it be?

"I was home-schooled by Mother and stayed inside for most of my life until a few years ago. Mother had it in her head that someone would kill me, so she kept me indoors."

Fran's eyes watered.

"Don't get upset," he said. "It was all I knew, and throughout my childhood, I had Cook and Milton."

She nodded as though she knew who they were. Of course she would. The police would have been nosing into Mother's friends and employees.

He wondered why Fran didn't ask who would want to kill him. Perhaps she already knew. That person who had talked might have said a few things more.

Cook, most likely. Or Milton.

"I'm a little backwards in most forms of social life, as you can imagine." He sipped from Thomas. "But it's all right, I manage well enough."

"Do you feel angry you were kept away from society?" Leona asked.

Ah, there it was, questioning to see if he had rage issues. Time to lie, much as it went against the grain, what with Mother's voice rattling in his ear about never telling fibs. "Oddly enough, no. If it's all you've known, you tend to get used to it. I'm happy to pop out every now and again, into the city, to see things, hear things I never did, but to be honest, I always feel better once I'm home. I bought a television the other day, you know. We've never had one before. I haven't set it up yet, but I'm interested to see what programmes are on offer. I bought a license and everything."

"No TV?" Leona appeared ready to self-combust with mortification on his behalf. "What about the radio?"

"Oh yes, I got to listen to that when Mother was out. Cook put it on when she taught me to bake and whatnot. She used to listen to sixties songs. I had a very secluded childhood, one I'm grateful for."

One I'm not *grateful for.*

"Well, that's something, at least," Fran said. "Can't say I wouldn't be raging angry if I were you."

He smiled gently, masking the very anger she'd mentioned. "Not me. I'm a quiet soul, and a quiet life is all I've ever wanted."

And, once the police stopped sniffing around and the other two were dead, a quiet life was what he'd have.

CHAPTER ELEVEN

Bethany and Mike had togged up and waited for the all clear to view the body.

The tent had been erected, the photographs of the deceased taken, and the Jeep hauled away to the lab. Isabelle gave them a wave, and Bethany and Mike joined her, Presley, and a few SOCOs inside, the halogen light stark on the old eyeballs after the sudden, late-afternoon murk that had descended outside. A storm was on the way, and darkness tiptoed into the sky, a stalker, itching to drench everyone in black.

SOCO, on hands and knees in the grass, searched for clues as quickly as possible out there before the rain came tumbling down and destroyed or compromised it all. Officers were doing the same inside, and a few markers dotted the area where skin and whatever had fallen onto the ground near the body.

Before they'd dipped into the tent, she'd been watching someone take a cast of divots over by the turbine pole. Two small holes, apparently. The SOCO reckoned they belonged to a bike stand. Parker's moped?

She sighed and walked closer to Cribbins, creeped out by the fact she'd seen him alive and well recently, if a little frosty and riddled with what she'd guessed was guilt. He'd been involved in this mess, no doubt about it, but why would someone want to kill him? Did he have a big mouth? Did he know who'd asked Parker to dig the hole and had to be kept quiet for good?

It wasn't lost on her that Parker had gone out on his moped, and divots from a bike were close by. They'd have to go round Parker's house again, find him, ask him where he'd been and why.

"He's had his face ruined by something like a rasp," Presley said, hunkering beside the body. "Is anyone on your radar a carpenter? A metal worker?"

"Joiner," Bethany said.

Mike came to stand beside her. "Who?"

"Aiden Parker. I noticed it on his file when Fran brought it up on her computer. What with the moped, I'm leaning towards him being the fucker who did this."

"Not surprising, given they were probably involved in the theft." Mike rubbed his chin with the back of his wrist. "Maybe Cribbins was on the verge of blurting to us. He seemed super edgy last time we saw him."

"Because he knew we were on to him, but obviously, I wouldn't have wanted this to happen to him." She stared at the wrecked face, nothing like how she remembered it.

"ID says it's John Cribbins." Isabelle put a wallet into an evidence bag. "And his phone is here in his pocket." She lifted it up and activated the screen — it must have one that accepted gloves on fingers. "Bonus, no passcode." She frowned over her face mask. "Hmm, someone rang him not long ago — whoever it is isn't in his phone contacts as it just comes up as a number. You'd think if it was the killer, they'd have deleted the log. What a douche."

Mike ferreted about unzipping his protective suit and brought out his notebook and pen. "Shoot."

Isabelle reeled the digits off, and he scribbled them down. Isabelle bagged the phone.

"Won't be a minute," Mike said and left the tent.

"Shit, hang on a sec!" Bethany legged it outside after him. "You'll have to ring Rob for the info. Don't forget I sent Fran and Leona round to Harry Allthrop's place about the things found in Margaret's car." She'd told him about those while they'd waited for the tent to be put up.

"Right you are." He dialled and walked away.

Bethany returned to the tent.

"There's such a mess in this eye socket, I can't see for the want of trying," Presley was saying. "Ah, ignore what I said. Maybe something sharp was stabbed into it — might be signs of the end of the instrument."

Isabelle leaned over to get a better idea of what he'd referred to. Bethany stayed where the hell she was. She didn't fancy seeing eye gore up close, thank you very much.

"As for the ear, something long and slim was rammed in there, several times by my reckoning," Presley said. "Whoever it was destroyed the earhole, in effect creating a bigger one, and if you have a peek, right . . . there," — he pointed to the side of the head — "you'll spot the fact that the weapon was also plunged into the temple, going upwards, and I'll lay odds that was what killed him. A spear to the brain has a habit of doing that, especially if it was a screwdriver or similar, as I'm suspecting."

"A bloody screwdriver?" Bethany said.

"Well, yes, it will be bloody." Presley grinned.

"You're sick, making jokes like that," Isabelle said. "Although to be honest, I'm actually pissed off I didn't come out with that myself."

"You two . . ." But Bethany smiled, then sobered. "All this over a sodding borer."

"Makes you think, doesn't it." Isabelle sighed. "Still, keeps us in a job. Criminals and the dead pay my wages. Now *that* was a quip and a half."

Bethany and Presley stared at her.

"Oh, come on now." Isabelle raised her eyebrows. "Tell me that was a good one."

They all laughed, rotten as it was, and some of the tension seeped out of Bethany. It seemed ages ago now that she'd almost wet herself in the car with Mike about Parker's neighbours. Was it really only earlier today? Christ, how a couple of hours changed things.

Mike came back in. "Pay-as-you-go, used in the city centre, pinged off the nearest tower, so we're shit out of luck. It's packed down there during the day, so spotting the user will be nigh on impossible."

"CCTV trawling it is then." Bethany blew out some air. "Poor Fran and Leona. Mind you, we could always get someone else to go through it. Long job, that, trying to find one person in amongst many."

"Want me to ring in and get someone on it?" Mike asked. "And who are we even looking for? Parker?"

"It's pointing that way, yes. Someone needs to also trace where that phone was purchased."

"Okay, back in a sec."

Off he went again, and Bethany tried to imagine what had gone down here. Cribbins had received a phone call — possibly from Aiden Parker using a burner. Whoever it had been, Cribbins must have either trusted them enough to meet them here or had been too frightened not to. He'd arrived; the killer was waiting. Maybe they'd talked, maybe they hadn't, but the result was a dead body and a killer who had no qualms about filing skin off faces and ramming screwdrivers into ears.

Who the fuck were they dealing with here? Okay, Parker had once been a joiner so might still have access to those tools. The bike stand divots. Parker going out on his moped. It had to be him, didn't it?

"We're going to have to go if there are no more clues as to who did this," she said to Isabelle. "We need to find Parker."

"Nope, nothing here." Presley smiled. "I sent you an email about Margaret Allthrop earlier, but I'll give you a recap. Now I'm seeing the gouges on this fella's face, it's brought something to mind. Margaret had her arse sliced off, yes? Well, around the edges of that slice are marks like these ones here. Come on, Beth, you really do need to see."

She stepped forward, holding her breath. Presley gestured to parts on the face that hadn't been totally ravaged, by the temple and on the edge of the cheek on the opposite side to the carnage. There were scrapes, as though the killer had used the file and gone in an upwards motion at those parts before going back to the main area and filing again.

"They are the same," Presley said.

"So the person who killed Margaret, killed Cribbins?" Bethany asked.

"Seems likely." Presley nodded.

"Why the hell would Parker bump Margaret off?" Bethany didn't get it. Unless Margaret had employed Parker for some reason and she'd upset him. She whipped her phone out, ringing Fran, hoping they were still at the Allthrop's.

"Hiya. On the way back to the station now," Fran said.

"Shit. How far away from Harry's are you?"

"Literally just left."

"Can you go back and ask him if his mother ever employed Aiden Parker?"

"Will do. In what capacity?"

"As a joiner, but you don't need to mention that."

"Leona, turn around and go back, love," Fran said. Then to Bethany, "What the heck is going on?"

Bethany gave her a quick burst of information. "So as you can see, we really need to get hold of Parker. He wasn't in when we called round there; he'd gone off on his moped."

"Ah, so the bike divots . . ."

"Exactly. I can't remember, but is Gina Fields John Cribbins' only family around here? All right, they're divorced, but you know what I mean."

"Yes, he's an only child, and his parents live abroad. Think it's Germany."

"Right, can you also sort letting them know their son's dead when you get back to the station? We'll go and see

Gina as a courtesy. Message me her address, there's a darling. Listen, I've got to go — oh, and Mike's sorting someone else to watch the city CCTV and trace the burner. Good job, really, because you two need to get back and seriously delve into Parker. Give me a ring when you're done with Harry."

"Okay, talk soon."

Bethany slid her phone away and waved to Isabelle and Presley, then left the tent in search of Mike. He was on his way towards her, and she jerked her thumb at the car.

"We need to go." She handed him her phone then went to work removing the protective clothing. "That's for when Fran rings if I'm driving. Come on, we need to go to Parker's again, see whether he's in."

See whether he's killed his mate and an elderly woman, the bastard.

* * *

Harry could scream. Someone was at the door again, and he'd only just got rid of the two detectives. He'd managed to get the TV out of the box and was about to set it up, but it would have to wait a while longer.

Fran and Leona stood there on the step, appearing apologetic.

Had this been their plan all along, to go away, let him think he was in the clear, only to come back and trick him?

"Oh, hello." He beamed at them. It hurt his face.

"We're so sorry to bother you again," Fran said, "but I forgot to ask a question."

"Come in then." He stepped back.

"No, no, I can ask it out here. It's not like you have any neighbours who'll earwig, is it." She smiled. "Did your mother ever employ an Aiden Parker to do any jobs around the house?"

Oh dear. Oh no. Where had they got that name from? And why had they associated the man with Mother? His neck grew hot, and if he wasn't careful, the heat would stretch up to his face, then they'd know something was wrong.

"Not that I know of. I do the accounts, and I certainly never paid anyone by that name."

"Thanks," Fran said. "We'll be off then."

He waved and shut the door as the flush sprawled all over his cheeks. Rushing to the kitchen, out of breath from the nudge of a panic attack, he leaned over the sink and splashed cold water on his skin. A few deep breaths later, he dried his face on the tea towel that he'd swiped off the jar.

The eyes stared at him accusingly.

"What are you lot looking at?" Harry said, waiting for a spiteful response.

None came, so he walked out and prepared to read the instructions on how to tune in a TV.

* * *

Harry stood in the corner of the walk-in fridge, his bare arms sticking out of his T-shirt sleeves, his banister-rail legs jutting from the hems of his shorts. Goosebumps sprouted, and he shivered. It had been a blessing to be locked in here at first after being caught running around the side garden with Milton in the sun, kicking a ball. He'd been so hot. Mother had dragged him in by his hair, muttering that Milton ought to scurry off and mind his own children instead of hers.

Harry was hungry, but he resisted eating anything. Mother might know; Cook certainly would — she had to keep a close eye on the food, otherwise, Mother took her to task. A bowl of runner beans sat on a steel shelf next to a large jar of pickled eggs. They'd be eyes if only they had irises. He pretended they were Mother's, plucked out of her head with the red screwdriver Milton had left on the table after fixing the kitchen windowsill.

His imagination knew no bounds, and it ran away, far into the distance towards Hell and all the evil it could muster, where Mother rambled around, sightless, arms out in front of her, feeling the air for Harry, to punish him for removing her soulless eyes.

His legs ached, so he sat on the floor, the chill of it seeping into his shorts and onto his skin. He peered to the back of the lowest shelf where Cook kept her stash of Coke and chocolates behind an orange box full of homegrown potatoes. Stomach growling, he closed his eyes to stop himself from reaching out and stealing a strawberry cream, maybe a caramel cup.

Lucky he didn't. The door flew open, and Mother stood there. As far back as he could remember, his most prevalent memory was her framed by a doorway, her silhouette, with the light behind her, morphing her into a monster.

"Go to The Study and think about what you've done," she said, as always.

He did as told, rushing upstairs and staring out of the window, rubbing warmth back into his arms. Milton stood by the rows of lettuces and stared up. Harry waved, and Milton glanced at the side door to the store grain, probably to see if Mother caught him interacting. Then he gazed at Harry and gave him a wiggle of his fingers. He pulled a face and raised his hands to flap his ears. Harry giggled and wished Milton would take him away from here.

"What's so funny?" Mother snapped behind him.

Harry whipped round. That silhouette again. That monster.

"I . . ."

"You're meant to be reflecting, not messing about with the staff," she said and brought the grater out from behind her back, whooshing it across his cheek.

The next time he went into The Study, a wooden board covered the window.

* * *

Bethany hammered on Parker's door for the fourth time. Annoyed he didn't — or wouldn't — answer, she stomped down the side of the house and opened the gate to the back garden. She walked in and approached the house. Flashlight out of her pocket, she shone it through the kitchen window — a clean and tidy interior, not a crumb on the worktop or a tea stain in sight.

Mike followed her a minute later. "He's not in. Weirdo Paul from next door just told me. He's been sitting at his window waiting for Parker to come back so he can ask him about the money he owes him."

"Then we'll nip to the Shank, see if he's there, celebrating the kill while establishing an alibi."

She drove them there.

No moped in the car park.

Rita was working, her pink eyeshadow fading. "He's not been in," she said. "Sorry."

Back in the car, while Mike flicked through his notes and mumbled to himself, Bethany stared out of the windscreen for a moment to gather her thoughts. An awful ache to be with Vinny crept inside her, bringing on the urgent need to cry. That happened sometimes, out of the blue, where all she wanted to do was sob until her tears dried out and her throat was sore.

Not today, grief.

Her message alert went off.

Thank fuck.

Fran: PARKER DIDN'T WORK AT THE ALLTHROP PLACE, SO HARRY SAID. ON ANOTHER NOTE, THE POLICE IN NUREMBURG ARE GOING TO TELL CRIBBINS' PARENTS ABOUT HIS DEATH.

Bethany: THANKS. PARKER ISN'T IN. HE ISN'T AT THE SHANK EITHER, SO WE'RE GOING TO NIP TO GINA FIELDS' PLACE AND BREAK THE NEWS ABOUT JOHN. CAN YOU CHASE UP WHETHER ANYONE PUT OUT A BOLO FOR PARKER? WE MIGHT GET LUCKY AND UNIFORMS SPOT HIM. ALSO CHECK ANPR, SEE IF THE MOPED CROPS UP.

Fran: OKIE DOKIE.

"Right, off to see an ex-wife," Bethany said.

"Oh, my favourite part . . . please note the sarcasm."

She smiled, and it lifted away some of the pain from where she'd wanted to see Vinny. Be with him. Hug him. Have him tell her everything would be all right, that she was strong and could do this thing called life without him. "Someone's got to do it."

"Yeah, it sucks to be us."

He didn't have a clue just how much she thought that about herself when lost in her darkest moments. It was certainly tough sometimes to be Bethany Smith, especially when she remembered she had another phone call to make before she could go anywhere.

To Tracy Collier of Serious Crimes.

Lovely.

She dialled.

"God," Tracy said, picking up after several rings. "Do we live in towns where residents like to murder or what? I've been briefed on what you're dealing with." She sighed. "What are you doing, checking in for the higher-ups so you can say we worked it between us that I'm not needed? Please tell me that's what you rang for, because I'm up to my effing tits in blood and gore here."

"Snap, and yes, this is just the courtesy call. We've got it under control, but you know if things go pear-shaped, I'll have to ask you to step in."

"Yep, fine, but for now, sod off."

The line went dead.

Bethany laughed almost as much as she had earlier with Mike.

Emotions. Swings and roundabouts, they were.

CHAPTER TWELVE

Before nipping to Gina Fields', Bethany drove to Selondra Imes' house, a posh affair on an avenue where people clearly valued giving out the impression that they were a cut above. Immaculate lawns, expensive cars, each home boasting its own Victorian streetlamp glittering on the driveways. Sadly, there was no answer, so she rang her, Mike reciting the number from the card Diana from the refuge had given them. Voicemail. They couldn't do much except keep trying periodically, so she drove them to their next destination. Selondra was only needed so they could get another side of Harry anyway, so seeing her wasn't pressing.

Gina Fields was a pretty sort, brunette hair in a low, messy bun, pink velour tracksuit covering a slender body that appeared to be put through it at the gym a few times a week. She carried tea over to them at her kitchen table and sat.

"I don't understand why anyone would want to do that to him," she said, voice hoarse after her crying jag, which had lasted the entire time she'd made the tea.

Funny how that happened. Divorced, couldn't stand him, yet still she'd cried. Maybe for the past and what they'd shared when it had been good, or, who knew, relief he was out of her hair for good.

"I know he must have pissed a fair few people off," Gina went on, "but to file off his *face*, for God's sake . . . Do you think it was Aiden?"

"We don't know at this time." It was best to say that. Saved Gina hurtling off trying to find the man, giving him a piece of her mind, possibly lashing out and getting herself into trouble.

Gina pursed her lips. "So, let me go over this again, what I heard on the telly."

On the telly?

"You suspect he was involved in the theft of a machine that cut holes, and someone ended up being killed and buried?" She blinked as if absorbing what she'd actually said. "Christ, that's just . . ." She shook her head. "What's the matter with people these days?"

"I think we'd all like to know that." Bethany smiled. "Then maybe we could get them the help they need *before* they kill anyone. Um, you mentioned the telly . . ."

"Yes, it's been on the news."

So Bethany hadn't had the chance to tell Gina a thing. The news had filled her in. They'd have to wait until they got back in the car to see what online had to offer by way of spilling information on their investigation. Apparently, it had gone out just before they'd arrived here, so Gina said. The thing was, with people walking dogs by the foot of the hill, word was bound to have leaked. Stupid to think it wouldn't, and now there'd be questions from the public, the phones ringing, and Kribbs, Fran, and Leona would have to give the standard answer of not being able to comment at this time.

"Do you think he'll come after me?" Gina asked, gaze darting between Bethany and Mike.

"I highly doubt it," Mike said. "You haven't had anything to do with this, so unless Aiden's got a problem with you . . ."

"Not that I'm aware of." Gina wiped her eyes with her sleeve. Mascara streaked the ribbed cuff.

That'll be a devil to get out.

They drank their tea for a while, Mike getting up to peer out into the small back garden. Bethany didn't need to move to see it in the low light, early evening encroaching even more now. Leaves had fallen from a large tree at the bottom, coating the grass in layers of red, yellow, and orange. Rain had fallen the second they'd stepped into Gina's, speckling the glass in the door and giving the leaves a sheen.

She thought of the SOCOs having to abandon their evidence search by the turbine if it continued to come down this hard.

Bethany's phone went off.

Fran: WARNING: THE CASE HAS LEAKED — PETER BLOODY UXBRIDGE FROM *THE SHADWELL HERALD* GOT HOLD OF IT. KRIBBS IS DEALING WITH THE PRESS CONFERENCE FOR YOU BECAUSE WE'VE HAD ANOTHER LETTER AND MAP.

What?

Bethany: OKAY, COMING RIGHT BACK.

Another letter and map meant another body. Did it have a picture of a Jeep and a big daisy for a turbine? Had Cribbins been found before the post had had a chance to get to them?

"I'm sorry, Gina, but we need to go." Bethany rose and gave a wan smile, adrenaline screaming at her to hurry this up and get going.

She said goodbye, left her card, and walked out, Mike jogging to keep up. She told him what was up in the car.

"Fucking hell . . ." He scratched his eyebrow. "Maybe it was delivered by hand this time and it's been sent for us to work out where Cribbins is."

"Seems that way."

They arrived at the station in short time and raced up to the incident room.

Fran got up and walked towards them with two A4 pieces of paper. "Photocopies — the real ones are at the lab."

"When did this come in?" Bethany asked, taking the map and letter.

"It was sent yesterday, according to the frank on the envelope."

"So why are we only just getting it now? It should have been here this morning." Had the killer sent it in advance, knowing he was going to kill Cribbins at Wind Energy? If so, whoever it was had taken a bit of a chance that Cribbins would actually agree to meet them there.

Fran shrugged. "Beats me. Either it came in the afternoon post, or the mail wasn't sorted here first thing."

Bethany went to Mike's desk and placed the papers down.

This map, to the right of a road, had a large smiley face beside what appeared to be a burger. On the left, a triangle had the words MEN AT WORK inside it, and away behind that, a dot. The road sign was a big fat alarm bell. She remembered the one found at Shadwell Hill. Had the killer bloody posed as a workman?

"Okay, roadworks," she said. "Get on that, Leona."

She read the note.

Dear Police,

I did a vile thing again. It's going to be a bit of a habit. You'll need a peg for your nose when you get there.

From,

Me

Bethany frowned. "So it must smell, wherever it is. Maybe meaning the body has been there a while, like Margaret? And what the hell is this smiley face about? Him laughing at us? I swear to you, when we find Parker, it'll take all my strength not to lump him one, fucking around with us like this."

"Somewhere in the city centre, perhaps?" Mike said. "A burger restaurant?"

"Fran, search for all the fast-food places that sell burgers for me, will you?" Bethany raked a hand through her hair, upset that there was a body out there and she couldn't get to it, couldn't give whoever it was some dignity by getting them down to the morgue as quickly as possible. "We don't want to spend forever on this scratching our heads like we did with the last map. Let's think outside the box this time. The flowers were turbines, so what if that's not a burger? What if that smiley face means something else?"

She paced, sifting through her mind for an answer. It wasn't playing ball and threw up blanks.

"Lots of roads with repairs going on," Leona called out. "None near fast-food."

"Bloody typical." Bethany said and looked at Mike. "Is this driving you mad like it is me?"

He nodded. "I don't like these games. What's the point of them?"

"Control," she said. "Calling the shots." Her office phone rang. "Bugger. Two secs." She rushed to answer it. "DI Smith."

"It's Rob. We've had a call from a farmer."

"And? Did a lamb go missing, trying to find Mary?" She closed her eyes and told herself off. "Sorry, we're a bit frazzled here. Been a long day."

"It's going to get longer, because it isn't about sheep. Or cows."

"Go on."

"It's a body."

"Oh, for . . ." She opened her eyes and studied the ceiling. "Okay, where is it?"

He gave her the details, and she ended the call. In the incident room, she wrote the address on the whiteboard — or as close as she could get, seeing as it was a field.

"Another body." She turned to face the team.

"Bloody hell," Leona said. "Overtime tonight then. Shall I order us some dinner?"

Bethany nodded. "Please. We'll have ours when we get back. Heat it up in the microwave." She got a twenty out and passed it over. "Anything will do, won't it, Mike?"

"Yeah."

"You can buy tomorrow's lunch and dinner, matey," she told him.

"Moped spotted on Four Peaks Road." Fran brought up a map on her screen. "Where's that body?"

"Four Peaks Farm . . ." Bethany realised what she'd said. "Shit! That fucker went there on his moped and killed somebody. Mike, we need to go. Fran, Leona, do your thing."

Bethany didn't even want to know what the time was. If she knew, she might cry. It had to be nearing the end of the official working day because her stomach rumbled.

She drove them to Four Peaks Farm in the now full dark, headlamps cutting through it. She parked outside the house. In the distance to the right, the SOCO van and a half-erected tent stood out, illuminated by a halogen. The area they were in was dark apart from an outside light beside the front door. Behind the house, slightly to the left, was a massive building, a one-story warehouse of sorts with a security light on above the door.

An age-beaten man came out of the house and approached — mucky jeans, dark-green jumper, black wellies caked in what might be shit — *nice* — and gave them a wave.

She showed him her ID and introduced them.

"You can take your car around the edges of the fields — that's how we don't ruin the crops or the ground," he said. "Each fence has a gap in it that links to the next field, and so on."

"Did you find the body?" she asked.

"No, the farmhand did, and he's still out there. He rang me, shitting bricks, and I called you lot."

"Thank you. Sorry to cut it short, but we need to get over there."

"By all means. I'm off to sort the cows."

They got back in the car, and Bethany followed the perimeters of the fields until she reached the SOCO van, parking behind it. She took their protective gear out of the boot, they got dressed, and then they headed for the officers who were almost done with putting up the tent.

"Bloody hell," Isabelle said, coming towards them. "I had to leave Cribbins' site to come here, leave today's team, and draft in tonight's early."

Bethany shook her head — killers didn't care that the police had to do overtime because of them. "What are we dealing with?"

"I haven't searched for ID as the photographer is still working, but it's a white male, and he's had his face ruined like Margaret and John." Isabelle folded her arms. "And there's a moped — it was shoved over the hedge into the next field, plus a helmet."

Bethany's heart lurched. Had Parker dumped it? Why?

"The lad who found the body is sitting over there." Isabelle jerked a thumb.

"Right, we'll go and speak to him now while the tent is still being sorted."

Bethany peered around, seeing no one in the darkness, then a shadow shifted. She got her torch out, switched it on, and led the way to a young bloke, blond, early twenties, face pale, arse parked on the grass in front of the SOCO van. No wonder she hadn't seen him when they'd arrived. He was almost hugging the vehicle. He lifted his head at their approach but remained sitting, as though he had no energy to stand.

Bethany crouched beside him and popped the torch down so it allowed her to see his face and him hers. "Hi. I'm DI Bethany Smith. What's your name, please?"

"Blake Olsten."

"I understand you found the body. Can you tell me what happened from the start?"

Blake closed his eyes and shuddered, then opened them again. "I was in the field behind us and saw the moped first. I was checking on the broccoli." He pointed to his flashlight beside him.

Mike peered over the hedge and squinted. "Learn something new every day. Broccoli in autumn! How can it survive in the cold?"

Blake smiled. "We have domes over them. We supply to one of the big supermarket chains." He sounded proud of that.

"What happened next?" Bethany asked.

"Well, I was walking the furrows, right down the far end, head bent, then made out something in the distance. It was just a black shape but something that shouldn't be there. I went over to it. Sometimes we catch people sleeping on the field edges in tents, but it was the moped, a helmet off to the side, and I wondered what the heck they were doing there. They'd been shoved over the hedge — I know that because the hedge was damaged. Kenny, that's my boss, he likes them all trimmed right, you know, straight lines. That's part of my job an' all, I do a bit of everything here, and I was miffed about part of the hedge being broken. Anyway, I peered over and . . ."

"Take your time."

"And saw *that.*" He pointed over at the now-erected tent, which glowed from the light within.

"What did you do?"

"I ran down to the nearest gap and came into this field. Onions grow here." He indicated the green leaves poking up through the soil, only visible in the circle of brightness from the halogen. "I didn't touch him; knew he was dead. So I rang Kenny, who told me to stay here, and that was hard. I mean, there's a dead bloke over there. Then you lot turned up."

"Did you stand close to the body?"

"Fuck, no. About three metres from it, then I kind of sidled past his feet, close to the hedge. Came and sat here. Haven't moved since, well, only to shift closer to this van."

"How long were you in the broccoli field for?"

"Only about ten minutes until I spotted the moped."

So it was unlikely he'd have been there when the man was being killed.

"Where were you before that?"

"Down in the sorting barn. There's loads of staff there who pack the veg after picking."

She peered back at the house, a black speck in the dark-grey distance. There were so many fields, and she doubted anyone would have seen a thing if they were inside. Still, she had to ask, "When you're in the sorting barn, is it likely someone in there would have taken a break and seen or heard anything?"

Blake shook his head. "It's well noisy in there, what with the machine that washes the produce, and breaktime had come and gone anyway. When I'm doing my walks of the fields, I listen to music," — he tapped his head either side — "earbuds, and like I said, I've got my head bent, inspecting the crops."

"Is it just you who does that job?"

"Nah, there's a few of us, but the other fields had already been done this morning. I got caught up helping in the sorting barn which is why I was late out here. Just my luck it was me doing broccoli today, eh?"

Bethany stood, picking up her torch. "Someone will take a formal statement from you, perhaps at home if you're more comfortable, or you can always go down to the station."

"I'll go in. Later tonight, all right?"

"That'll be fine, or the morning. Thanks for going through that with us. You should go home."

Blake peeked at his watch. "Should have been home over an hour ago." He got up and switched on his torch. "See you."

She watched him trudge off, past the van, then her car, the shaft of light bobbing with each step, which was then swallowed up by headlamps coming their way.

"Ah, here's Presley."

The ME's red car rumbled down the edge, stopping a few metres behind Bethany's. That was good. She was about to wave at him to back off so he didn't block her in. As it was, she'd have to reverse alongside his vehicle to get out so she didn't drive on the part of the field used for the onions.

Presley put on his protective clothing then walked up to them. "I'd just left the turbine scene, got back to the lab, and no sooner had I washed up ready to carry on with Margaret's PM than I was called out again. This lark is becoming a habit."

"Know what you mean."

"Thankfully, someone else will take Cribbins in once forensics have finished there and he can be moved," he said.

While they walked to the tent, Bethany got her phone out to see the time. Bloody hell . . . Coming up to six-thirty.

"Ah, there you are," Isabelle said. "He has ID."

"Well, that's something." Bethany stood beside the body but didn't study it. Not just yet. "Seems the killer doesn't mind us knowing who these people are."

"I found a phone on the grass, though, so maybe he was holding it and dropped the thing. Killer doesn't seem bothered about that either." Isabelle shrugged. "Anyway, your theory on the killer's identity is up the swanny now."

Bethany stopped herself from groaning. "Go on, give it to me."

"This," Isabelle said, sweeping her arm out in the body's direction, "is one Aiden Parker."

CHAPTER THIRTEEN

"Where the hell does that leave us now?" Bethany said. "So, did the killer arrange to meet him here like they did with Cribbins?" She didn't expect answers. It was obvious what had happened. Someone else had probably rung Cribbins — it couldn't have been Parker — and they were searching for a grain of salt in a kid's ball pit.

Fucking great.

"The borer theft links all three people," Mike said, "so we go from there."

"*Where* do we go, though? We've known it links them from the start, and we've no direction now Parker's dead." Bethany couldn't think straight. Today had been one thing after another, and she was tired, verging on exhausted, not to mention hungry as eff.

Isabelle's phone tinkled. She pulled it out and accessed her email. "Ah, an update from the lab on the soil in the hole. Margaret *was* down there. Hairs, skin, and urine were picked up, all hers."

"Jesus. I wonder how long she was down there," Bethany mused. "With the energy bars, I'd say a while, but why bother feeding her if you're going to kill her?"

"Maybe to give her hope she'd be kept alive. A sick joke." Mike sighed. "Who knows. Mind games? I mean, let's be honest here, whoever did this is playing with us, otherwise, why go to all the trouble with the letters and maps?"

That reminded Bethany, and she updated Isabelle about the second delivery.

"So we have another body to come, because there's no smiley face or a bloody burger around here, nor any Men at Work signs," Isabelle said.

Bethany nodded. "Maybe the next body will make it clearer who's doing this. A closer link to Margaret, perhaps, so we've got more to go on."

"Unless we get lucky and they're being kept alive in another hole," Mike offered. "That might be why the borer wasn't returned — they hadn't finished with it yet."

"Unlikely. We have three bodies already. This person doesn't seem the type to let anyone go free." Bethany pushed out a breath. "Right, let's have a butcher's at this poor sod then, shall we?"

She shifted her gaze to Parker. His face had also been scraped away. Fat, muscle, and ripped flesh sat proudly, raw mincemeat. Bethany wouldn't be making a chilli or spag bol in the near future, not until she'd forgotten this sight. One of his eyes was missing, and that had to mean something, as all of them had been left the same way. At least they had a few things to mull over:

No eye.

Fucked-up cheeks.

A screwdriver.

A filing tool.

They had to mean something to the killer.

"If someone had driven here in their car, surely they'd have been seen," she said. "On foot, well, that'd take a while to walk here and back to wherever they live, unless it was someone who works here. We'll have to go and speak to the farmer, get a list of employees. We might have to talk to them all. Christ, that's a mountain to climb if ever there was one. Got an estimate on the time of death?" she asked Presley.

He was busy peering into the eye cavity. "Hours ago, but today, after lunch. Same instrument used to take the eye out and stab the ear. Well, might not be the exact same one, but it's a similar weapon. Screwdriver or the like."

Bethany sighed out her frustration, said goodbye, and messaged Fran to send her the next of kin for Parker, explaining it wasn't him they were after now. Then she drove to the farmhouse, where they took off their gear outside and stuffed it into a paper evidence bag in the boot.

Kenny must have finished with the cows. He walked towards them from a field on the left. To have livestock and run a veg farm, he must be one hell of a busy bloke.

"Want a brew?" he asked, sounding as weary as Bethany felt.

Should they? It would fill the hole created by hunger, stop her chewing her arm off to shut her stomach up. "Please, that would be lovely." She baulked at his shit-caked wellies and hoped he'd wash his hands before making them a drink.

They trooped into the house, Kenny leaving his wellies by the door, and he went to a modern kitchen that was at odds with her expectations for a farmhouse. She'd imagined pine cupboards and a scarred table, a dish on the side containing real butter, and a bowl full of fruit, maybe some chintz curtains with pelmets and the standard Collie lounging in front of a roaring fire. Instead, it was minimalist — and extremely white. Glaring.

Bethany and Mike sat on stools at a shiny island, and Kenny thankfully scrubbed his hands then worked the pod machine to make coffee, yapping all the while about it being a shame someone was dead.

"I need to ask about your employees." She had to interrupt else she reckoned he'd be chatting all evening. "How can you be sure none of them left the sorting shed — unless you were in there, too, that is?"

"Because they can't get out of the door without using their individual keypad codes, and when they do, it registers on my app, and I get a bleep on my phone. A bit extreme, but I've had staff bunk off in the past so decided to take measures. I pay for them to work, not have a fag round the bloody corner or dick about on Facebook on their mobiles."

Vinny's voice floated in her head: *That's a fire hazard, sweetheart. People could get trapped.*

She swallowed down emotion — Christ, he'd been clear as day — and asked, "So what happens in the event of a fire?"

Mike gave her a sad smile and squeezed her hand under the island.

"I'm okay," she said, voice low.

The machine gurgled, hopefully hiding what she'd said from Kenny, and he removed one cup from beneath the spout then added another. While he poured cream from a jug and sorted sugar, clearly assuming they wanted it, he said, "Once the fire alarm goes off, the door locks disengage. A bit like a sprinkler system works — automatic."

That made her feel a bit better. "Tell me about the day-to-day running of this place."

"Sorting in the shed is from nine till five." — *Dolly Parton* — "The field rounds are usually done in the morning, but I needed Blake to help with the sorting today, so the broccoli was left until later. Blake was the only one out of the building in the field at that time, except for me, and I was on the phone in here to the bloke at Sainsbury's, working out a better price for the veg. I tell you, that was a struggle and a half. It took me an hour for him to agree, and I finished just as Blake rang about the body. Everyone else had gone home. My supervisor locked up the shed. I'd accessed the app before they buggered off, though, and it was fine — no one except Blake had left since lunch, so they must have remained in there to have their afternoon tea break."

"And all staff were present today? No one off sick?"

Kenny shook his head.

In one way, it was a relief not to have to question multiple employees, but in another, it meant they had no eyewitnesses or a suspect. Like she'd said earlier, no direction.

Kenny brought their coffees over and placed them on the island, then went back to make his.

"Thanks," Bethany said, taking a sip and thinking this was the closest she was going to get to utopia today — unless Leona ordered something bloody gorgeous for their dinner.

"Lovely," Mike said.

"Blake told us it's unlikely anyone would have heard a vehicle," Bethany said.

Kenny nodded, carrying his coffee to the island and then sitting. It seemed he was glad to take the weight off his feet, the poor sod. He sighed and closed his eyes for a moment. "He's right. I'd take you in there so you'd know the level of noise, but all the equipment is shut down. Put it this way, some of them wear earplugs. It's that big building out the back there. It's not only the washer that's loud, but the other machines. They can grumble a bit."

She thought about it being Blake then dismissed it. Presley had mentioned Parker being dead for hours. Regardless, she said, "Can you show me this app to see when Blake exited the sorting shed?"

Kenny got his phone out, pressed a blue icon, scrolled, and turned the screen towards her. "There. Four-fifteen. It takes a good twenty minutes to get to the broccoli on foot, then he'd walked down a few furrows before he spotted the moped, so he'd said. He'd have used his torch as it was getting well dark by then."

"Thank you." Nowhere near lunchtime as Presley had predicted.

She changed the subject then, and they discussed the farm until the coffee cups were empty. Kenny asked when he'd get his field back, and Bethany gave him Isabelle's number so he could sort it with her. There was no telling how long they'd be out there.

With goodbyes and thanks said, Bethany walked alongside Mike to the car. Once seated, she let out a groan, her muscles as weary as her brain. Nevertheless, there was still work to be done, so she rang Selondra Imes again, and with no answer, left a message for her to get in contact with them as soon as she was available. Call cut, she pressed her message icon. Fran had got back to her with a next of kin.

"One more stop, then back to the station," she said and drove off.

Mike blew a raspberry — she laughed at that — and he leaned an elbow on the doorframe. "What a day."

"You're telling me. Fran's given me the address of Parker's mum, so we'll have to deal with weeping before we can go and get some grub."

"Dropping that news on an empty stomach . . ."

"I know. Dropping it on a full one isn't much better."

Once again, they ended up on Shadwell Heights — damn place — the next street along from Parker's. A light burned inside number twenty, and Bethany knocked. The poor woman had no idea her life was about to be ruined. She had a few seconds of ignorant bliss before she opened that door, then the worms of unease would act up in her belly once she knew coppers stood there.

The door suddenly gaped before them, pulled sharply by a lady in her late fifties, face like a slapped arse, grey-blonde hair hanging in lank rivulets, chip fat city. "What?" she said, sounding more like *wot*.

Bethany did the usual with her ID and told her who they were. "We need to come in."

"If that son of mine — who won't answer his fucking phone, I might add — has done something illegal, you can piss off out of it. I don't want anything to do with that sort of bollocks."

"Mrs Parker—"

"It's Raleigh, and *Miss* not Mrs — I didn't marry no bugger. Men are all the same. Wasters and users, the lot of them, including Aiden."

Bloody hell . . . "Miss Raleigh, if you'd just let us in . . ."

"Oh, pissing well come in then. No point arguing with you lot, is there." She stomped off down the hall.

Bethany stared at Mike. He was on the verge of laughing, and it had her wanting to do the same.

"Don't," she whispered, "or I'll make *you* deal with her."

She went in and found *Miss* Raleigh in the living room, arse in a brown velvet chair, legs propped up on a matching pouffe. She'd lit a cigarette, and the smoke writhed towards the ceiling. The room was a right old shit state, and Bethany was glad they'd already had a coffee at Kenny's. She wouldn't want to drink out of any mug here. She didn't want to sit either so stood by the window. Mike remained near the doorway, appearing uncomfortable in the scummy surroundings.

Best to get this over and done with so they could escape pretty sharpish. The smell of that cigarette was foul, as was the underlying stench of mould.

"What's your relationship like with your son?" Bethany asked so she could get a measure of how the woman would take this.

"He's a pest, always in trouble, and always doing something he shouldn't. Can't stand the prat. He's just like his father, he is."

"If you can't stand him, why were you trying to ring him?"

"Because I've had that bloody Paul on my doorstep, haven't I, asking me for his wages. How am I meant to give them to him? I'm on the bleedin' dole. And why should I, anyway? It's between Aiden and Paul, nothing to do with me. So I was ringing him to give him an ear-bashing and tell him once and for all to sod off out of my life. It'll be much nicer without him in it, not that I see him from one month to the next, but still."

Okay then . . .

"I'm sorry to have to tell you that your son's body was found this evening." Bethany held her breath.

Raleigh roared with laughter and flicked her fag ash in a saucer on a magazine and crumb-covered table. "Oh, that's poetic justice, that is. Someone's killed him, have they?"

"Why would you automatically think that?" Mike's head snapped up, and he paused from writing in his notebook.

He'd probably been logging her reaction in case they needed it for future reference.

"Because he's always got someone or other after him. You pinch things round here, people are likely to think he did it — he's known for it, see, just doesn't get caught by the likes of you. This isn't a surprise to me at all."

"You're not upset." Bethany waited for some other emotion to kick in that would show Raleigh had even a smidgen of feeling for her child.

"D'you know what? No. He's been a royal pain up my arse ever since he could walk and talk. One thing after another — every day there was something. When he nicked my TV and laptop, that was it for me. He's a damn loser."

There was no point in offering for the FLO to come round. Seemed it would be a waste of time and resources. With nothing more forthcoming from Raleigh when Bethany asked several questions, they took their leave.

On the drive to the station, Bethany said, "What the actual?"

"I suppose that tells us some people really can dislike their children. Not an ounce of sorrow in her — unless she's the stoic sort and held it together until we left."

"I don't know. She honestly didn't seem bothered by it, other than to gloat that he'd got his comeuppance, but really, does a small-time thief deserve that?"

Mike shook his head. "I don't think I'll ever forget the way she took the news."

Bethany wondered if he was thinking about how *she'd* taken it regarding Vinny. Her scream from that day sometimes rang in her head at random times, and in her nightmares, full of such agony she could barely breathe in remembrance. When she'd had the arse ripped out of her world, it was no surprise she'd wailed like that — and a few times since.

Thank God they were at the station now so she didn't have to entertain that train of thought anymore. They walked into the incident room, greeted by the smell of curry, and Bethany's tummy griped.

"Hi, you two," she said, going over to Mike's desk to peer inside the brown takeaway bag on it. Cutlery and two plates had been brought up from the canteen. While she dished up, she went through what had been happening so Fran and Leona were on the same page. She popped Mike's food in the microwave for a couple of minutes — chicken tikka by the looks of it, while she had a korma — and asked if they had any news.

Fran nodded. "CCTV in the city obviously didn't bring up Parker, and now we don't know who we're searching for, it was basically nameless faces in crowds for the officers dealing with it. Once you'd let me know the recent body is Parker's, I sorted out the collection of his Transit. Forensics said the borer was found and will be analysed for soil deposits that match the hole. SOCO have gone round to his house — only a couple of them, obviously, what with the rest being at the Cribbins and Parker scenes — to do the usual there."

"Leona?" Bethany smiled at her.

"ANPR threw up a few cars heading towards Four Peaks Farm in several directions, but it led to nothing because those cars continued on and were spotted resuming their journey with no time for stops in between to murder someone. I've stuck a map on one of the whiteboards and studied it to see where the killer could have come from." She got up and walked over there.

Bethany took Mike's meal out of the microwave and carried it over to him. She popped hers in next. "Before I forget, do I owe you any more for this food?"

"Six-ninety," Leona said. "So, here's Four Peaks Farm." She jabbed a finger on the map. "It's three and a half miles away from Shadwell, and the amount of houses lining the road where the city starts is unreal — lots of locations where the killer could live. However, Harry Allthrop's place is *three* miles away, the closest building to the farm in that direction, to the right. As you can see, the fields of the farm butt up to his property, so he could have walked there, offed Aiden, then walked back. I've Googled this, and at moderate speed, we're at twenty minutes to the mile, so an hour to get there, an hour to get back. But if he jogged, it's about eight to ten minutes per mile, but that's someone in pretty good shape. He didn't strike me as a man up on his fitness."

Bethany agreed. "So if it was him, it would be two hours of walking altogether, plus the kill time, for Aiden. Presley estimated his death after lunch, so let's call it two o'clock. That would mean Allthrop would be home past four, given however long it took to commit the murder. And that takes us to *after* Cribbins died — and he used the Jeep to get to the turbine at about three. If Allthrop ran to the field, we're talking a more reasonable timeframe. Which brings up the question: If we think Allthrop's the one we're after, he must have a bike — unless the divots at the turbine aren't from a kickstand. The moped was left at Parker's scene, so he didn't use that to get home or to Wind Energy."

The microwave dinged, and she took her food to the spare desk and plonked her backside down. Her feet throbbed, and it brought Kenny to mind when he'd sat with immense relief.

"What about in the other direction?" she asked.

Leona moved her finger past the farm to the left. "Here, there are houses dotted along Winton Road, few and far between, and I've rung the residents. All were at work except one, and I took down their employment addresses to verify that tomorrow. The only person indoors at the time of the murder was an old man, and he joked he wouldn't be able to get over the fields in his wheelchair. I did a search on him, and he's eighty-four, disabled, so that's him ruled out."

"Okay, what about the second map we got sent? Anything on the pictures that were drawn?" God, this food was lush. She could eat korma all bloody day — it was that nice. Her belly had finally stopped moaning, which was a bonus.

"No, afraid not," Fran said.

"You two may as well call it a day then." Bethany ate some more curry.

"I might just get back in time to put the little one to bed." Fran smiled.

“Sorry you sometimes don’t see her much.” Bethany felt guilty about that.

“My choice of career, so don’t even think about feeling bad.”

Fran and Leona shut down their computers and left.

“Right then, matey,” Bethany said to Mike. “We’ll have a quick squiz at the news, see what that *Herald* prat had to say, then shoot off ourselves. You staying at mine again?”

“If you want me to.”

“Yep. Don’t fancy being by myself.”

“Then let’s do this and hurry up about it. There’s a beer in your fridge waiting for me.”

CHAPTER FOURTEEN

MARGARET ALLTHROP — DEAD!
PETER UXBRIDGE: REGIONAL CRIME

Margaret Allthrop, our local 'celebrity', was found buried at the foot of Shadwell Hill. A source close to the police stated: "She'd been kept in a cylindrical hole, perhaps for several days, with only energy bars and a flask of fluid. Her face had been marked, and one eye was missing. Another part of her was also missing. It was an awful sight and no way to go for anyone."

She is survived by her son, Harry Allthrop. Margaret is known for her donations to the women's refuge, her help there, and her passion for ensuring the women and children segue into a life free from anxiety and worry, and above all, that they are safe. She was an avid charity lover and a staunch feminist.

Our contact also said: "This was a particularly brutal murder, and she'd been found through communication with the killer, who'd sent a handwritten letter and a crudely drawn map, which indicated where her body had been left. However, with the directions somewhat obscure, it took a few days to locate her."

Someone out there knows who this person is. That person would have been covered in blood, has perhaps been acting strangely over the past week or two, and may well be exhibiting signs of distress or euphoria. If you think a family member or friend fits this behaviour, please contact Shadwell station.

"We've got a fucking leak," Mike said. He clicked to close the browser.

Bethany's blood boiled. "We have indeed. It could be anyone — but not Fran or Leona, I refuse to believe that. Maybe it's someone from Isabelle's team. That bit about the body being in an awful state — it's got to be an officer who was there, unless they have access to the crime scene photos."

"Hmm. Whoever it is ought to pack it in. Giving out these sorts of details isn't on, is it. Talk about potentially fucking things up."

"I'm going to ring that Uxbridge git and ask him outright." She accessed his number in her phone from when she'd stored it during the Bishway case and called him, expecting argumentative responses, as was his way. Well, he'd damn well get argumentative back, the tosser.

He answered quickly, probably sitting there at home smiling at her name popping up, pleased his article had warranted her ringing him at this time of night instead of waiting until the morning. "To what do I owe this pleasure, DI Bethany Smith, as if I can't guess?"

"Who gave you that information?" Right out with it, no messing. She was too steamed up to go at it lightly.

"Oh, naughty, naughty. You know I can't divulge that." Smarmy.

"Can't or won't?" Aggravated.

"Won't." A chuckle. "I was asked to keep it under my hat for obvious reasons."

"If they said that, then they know damn well what they did was wrong — and *you* know better than to do this."

"I chase stories. It's my job. *I* contacted *them*, all right? They just . . . gave me the information while in general conversation. You could almost say it slipped out. An 'oops' moment on their part, as it were."

She could punch him. Honestly. "I suppose you'll tell me next you promised it was off the record, then you had an 'oops' moment of your own and 'forgot' you were meant to keep it to your bloody self. I don't believe that for one second. As you know, this sort of thing can seriously derail a case. What if we were holding the information back for a reason?"

"Clearly not, otherwise I wouldn't know it, would I."

God, he was a cocky bastard.

"In future, please do *not* print anything about murder investigations unless it comes from Chief Kribbs or me, understand? If you do, I'll have to make sure you're properly reprimanded for it."

"Blah-blah-blah. You can't do anything to me."

He cut the call.

"He just bloody hung up on me!" She gawped at Mike, mouth hanging. The urge to scream crept in, and she forced it back. "Of all the . . ."

Mike rested a hand on her shoulder, his face showing how concerned he was. "Don't let him piss you off. He enjoys the reactions he gets. I bet he's imagining it now, how steaming you are, and laughing to himself. You know what he's like."

"But all the same, I can't help but get riled up when he's involved." She put the takeaway bag in the bin for something to stop her from ringing that twat again and having a complete mare at him. "We should watch the press conference, really, see what was said. It must have gone out on the news by now."

Mike brought up a browser and found what they wanted. Kribbs sat behind a table in his uniform, a white wall behind him, a microphone in front.

"What do you have to say about Mrs Allthrop?" an unseen journalist asked.

Christ, give him a chance to issue the statement first.

Kribbs turned to his left. "All we can divulge at this time is that the body of Margaret Allthrop was discovered at Shadwell Hill. She had been murdered."

"Is it true what's in *The Herald*?" someone else said — a woman.

"I'm not prepared to release details at this time," Kribbs said.

"But *some*one did," another blurted.

"We will be looking into that." Kribbs appeared uncomfortable — and annoyed. His face coloured, and he fiddled with his tie as if it had suddenly become too tight. "Information such as this shouldn't be taken seriously unless it comes from me or my staff in a conference."

Bethany smiled. "There you go. That's the way to discredit Uxbridge and his source in one sentence."

Cameras flashed and clicked. Kribbs blinked.

"So you're saying the information isn't true?" came the voice of that bloke from *Sky News*.

"That's all for now." Kribbs rose and went out of shot.

Mike tutted. "Bloody sharks."

"Yes, until they're useful to us, and they are sometimes, just not today. I'm sick of Uxbridge doing this sort of thing. I can't stand him."

"Not many people can. Time to go home then?"

"Yep. You should keep some clothes at mine, you know, so I don't have to keep dropping you at yours to pick them up. Or, failing that, just bloody well move in."

Had she really said that?

Mike stared at her. "What?"

"You may as well." Yes, now she thought about it, it made sense. They got on, he respected her need for privacy, and Vinny would be smiling now if he were here, egging her on to pursue this. She was lonely. Mike was lonely. "It'd save us both money. We could split everything down the middle."

He frowned. "Won't people think . . . ?"

"I don't give a toss what they think. Do you? Really?"

He grinned. "No. We're mates. People live with their mates, don't they."

"Okay, well, whenever you're ready." She aimed to change the subject before she got choked up. The relief at having someone at home with her all the time was massive. She wouldn't be so isolated on the nights Mike didn't stay now. "Let's get going. Like you said, that beer's waiting."

* * *

She decided to drive them past the Allthrop place, just to see if anything was off. As they didn't have anything on him, they couldn't bring him in based on the fact he happened to live closer to the farm than anyone else. They could visit him tomorrow on the pretext they were asking after his welfare, seeing as his mother's death had been splashed all over the news. Actually, sod it, she'd stop in the lay-by just here and give him a call.

"What are you doing?" Mike asked.

"Ringing Harry quickly. If it's him, we'll at least have it logged that we made contact once we found out about the distance between his house and the farm — okay, we're late in doing so, but do you see where I'm going with it?"

"Yep. Covering our arses. Saves any questions being asked later. Do you really think it's him?"

"It's best to be safe. Me speaking to him now will let him know, if he's the one we're after, that we're not going away."

She dialled Harry's landline, and he picked up almost immediately.

"Hello, Harry Allthrop speaking." Plum in his mouth.

"Harry, it's DI Bethany Smith. How are you?"

"Not too bad, considering. Thank you for asking."

"Have you seen or heard the news today? I'm ringing to make sure you're all right."

"I haven't, no. I didn't put the radio on, and I've set my new TV up but haven't watched it yet. Has Mother's death been reported?"

"Yes, and I'm afraid some information has been picked up, so it may be distressing for you to read or watch. I advise you to avoid it. What have you been up to? Anything interesting to take your mind off things?" She hoped she sounded conversational and not like she was fishing.

"I had a couple of visits from your colleagues. That was nice. They're a lovely pair."

"Yes, they are. What else did you do?"

"As I said, I set up my TV, pottered around. Nothing of much importance. As you can imagine, it's strange here without Mother. I'm not sure I'll ever get used to it."

"I can imagine. I just need to ask . . . Did you by any chance see out of a window at all and spot anyone in the fields behind your house? I appreciate they go a fair way back and seeing someone in the distance might be nigh on impossible."

"No, I didn't, I'm afraid. Why do you ask?"

"It doesn't matter. I'd best be off. I'll ring you or come to see you tomorrow at some point, make sure you're bearing up."

"That's very kind of you, but there's no need. I'll be fine. I'd rather you concentrate on finding Mother's killer than mollycoddling me. Goodnight."

The second time being cut off in one evening left her open-mouthed again. She should make allowances for the fact he was grieving. After all, she hadn't wanted anyone bothering her either; she'd do well to remember that sooner before pushing people.

"Did you sense anything?" Mike asked as she pulled out of the lay-by.

"No. He hasn't got a clue about the news."

"Ouch if he sees it."

"Yep."

She drove on into the darkness, thinking about how she'd coped with Vinny's death being reported. It had waxed lyrical about his heroic actions, and while what he'd done trying to save that baby's life was beautiful, she'd hated reading those words — because they'd highlighted *why* he was no longer here. *Why* she was a widow.

Fuck it.

On the lonely road past Harry's house, to her right, a square of light behind it in the distance meant SOCO were still in Kenny's field. Things may well go on into the early hours there, officers walking the furrows for evidence.

"Are you thinking too much?" Mike asked, ever watchful of her state of mind if she went silent for extended minutes.

They had been friends and partners for so long, she was hard pressed to remember a time he hadn't been in her life.

"I was," she said. "Not now, though. Thanks for . . . well, you know, being here."

"It's what friends do."

"I'm going to disturb your sleep more than a few times a week when you move in," she said. She had nightmares, where she followed Vinny into the burning house and watched him die holding that baby's hand through the cot bars. She tried to pull him out, but he was always too heavy, and her heartbreak at having to leave him there so she didn't die herself tore her to pieces. She woke sweating, guilt-ridden, and tearful. Many a time, Mike had come in to sit on the edge of her bed until she managed to fall back to sleep.

He was a friend and a half. One in a million.

"Don't take this the wrong way, but I love you dearly," she said.

"I know. Kind of love you, too. Now piss off being soppy."

They laughed.

A couple of miles had flown past and, in another lay-by, a static food van came into view. If she hadn't had that curry and the place was open, she'd have stopped and grabbed them a burger and chips. She sailed past.

Mike shouted, "Stop!"

Her heart hammered from the shock of his voice being so loud, and she slammed on the brakes. "What the fuck?"

"Go back. To the van."

She reversed, hands shaking, manoeuvring to park to the left side of the static, her headlights splashing on it, showing up filth that must have coated it from passing traffic. The front hatch was shut, then she lowered her gaze to beneath it.

"Fuck me . . ." she said, staring at Mike.

"The smiley face." He blinked.

Next to it in swirly font: SMILE AND EAT!

She felt sick. Adrenaline pumped, leaving her light-headed. "We'd best get our gear on, just in case." She grabbed them an outfit and gloves each from the box in the back seat, handing Mike his. "Actually, I'd better reverse onto the roadside and put the hazards on. If this is what we think it is, we'll need the scene clear."

She did that, then they exited and dressed quickly.

"Ugh, can you smell that cow shit?" she asked.

"Maybe that's what the note meant about having a peg on our noses."

"Hmm."

Large torch from the boot in hand, she approached the van, Mike beside her, going to the right. The beam picked out the tip of a road sign amongst the brush, the yellow of it bright. She leaned forward and parted the dried foliage, exposing the words she'd been dreading yet had wanted to see: MEN AT WORK.

"This is it," she said. "We've bloody well found it."

Mike turned his face to the sky. "The dark is going to hamper us."

"Then they'll have to use the fucking chopper if we don't see anything. The dot on the map was behind this sign. I'm reluctant to go tramping through here into the field in case we stand on the burial spot and mess things up." She pointed her beam farther right. "Actually, there's a lamppost there." It wasn't working. "Help me get up it."

"What?"

She headed that way. "You can give me a leg up, and I'll hang on to it if you stay below and hold my legs."

Mike shook his head. "All right."

They walked over there, and Mike gave her a boost, fingers laced. She hoisted herself up and hugged the pole with one arm and directed her beam into the field. On the other side of the scrubby brush that ran along the grassy edge was a dip, which lowered into a ploughed field. She swung the light back and forth, side to side, then stopped. About a metre out was a mound.

"Okay, I think I've found it. Same sort of resting place as Margaret. You can let go of me now." She slid down the pole.

Mike got on the phone, and while he talked, she had a nose about. The back of the static didn't have windows, so whoever ran this place wouldn't have seen the grave in the daylight. It was clear they hadn't seen it while getting in and out of their vehicle either — probably too intent on starting work, then later, going home.

Mike came up to her. "Isabelle is on her way. SOCO have finished at Wind Energy, and only a small team has been left at Four Peaks. God, you've got to feel sorry for them lot coming out again, haven't you."

"Um, excuse me, mister. Isabelle has three teams on rotation. And what about us? We're here, too."

"I suppose. It's going to be a long one, isn't it."

"Yep, we'll be home well past midnight at this rate. It'll take them a while to unearth the body."

Isabelle and some of her team arrived, and while they got to work, Bethany and Mike sat in the car after putting up a cordon. A uniform arrived, so Bethany got out again to brief him.

Glen Underby strode up to her. "Evening, boss."

"Evening to you, too. On shift already, were you?"

He nodded. "Do you want me directing traffic?"

"Please. Take down their names and plates. Some people like coming back to the scene of the crime. You can get started straight away." She gestured to behind him.

He trotted off, stopping the vehicle and speaking to the driver.

Bethany sat in the car again, her feet absolutely killing her.

"I rang the front desk for Ursula to find out the owner of this van," Mike said.

"Let's hope she isn't already having a busy time of it then. If she gets back to you soon, we can go and visit the owners while we wait for things to get moving here."

On cue, his phone beeped.

"Back to Shadwell Heights," Mike said on a sigh.

"Pissing Nora."

They removed their gear, putting it on the rear seat. She flicked the hazards off and drove towards Glen, who'd sent the other vehicle back the way it had come. Window down, she called out, "Can you shout into the field and let Isabelle know we've gone to question the static owner?"

"Will do."

"Thanks."

She set off, weary but oddly hyper at the same time, wondering whether the person they were going to see was thick enough to kill then dump the body behind their place of work. A thought struck her then. "We're close to Harry's place."

"Hmm."

"What do you reckon?"

"It's suss."

"It is. The thing is, we need proof, and so far, we've got nothing."

"Story of our working lives."

"You can say that again."

CHAPTER FIFTEEN

The call from Bethany Smith unsettled Harry, to the point he fretted, thinking she was onto him, and that she knew what he'd done. She'd been kind in enquiring after his well-being, but what if it hadn't been about that? In the time since the conversation, he'd been trying to work the blasted TV, but his mind wasn't on the job. It came with the internet, and it had taken him a good twenty minutes to figure out how to access a news page. The instructions had seemed too complicated for him to fathom.

He should have taken Smith's advice and avoided it.

Details of Mother's state had been mentioned, bringing home to him what he'd done. While he'd been filled with rage, grating her face, gouging out her eye, and enjoying hurting her like she'd hurt him, it had been the right thing to do, but now . . . he felt ashamed. To see it all in black and white, there on a page filling his TV . . .

But she deserved it. She was wicked. Evil. All of them deserve it.

He had to remind himself of that. Of how bad things had been. Otherwise, with it hammered into him all his life to always tell the truth, he might just confess during a weak moment, and that wasn't allowed. Not while there was still work to be done.

He was The Avenger.

* * *

Harry, celebrating his eighteenth birthday, walked into the kitchen to view the cake Cook had made. She'd gone all out, baking three layers — one chocolate, one vanilla, and one lemon, so she informed him, all his favourites. She beamed at him, standing behind the beautiful creation that sat on the table in front of her. Thomas the Tank Engine stood on a track on the bottom layer, the Fat Controller on the middle, and the station on the top.

Perfect.

"Do you like it?" Cook wrung her hands and bit her bottom lip.

Milton was beside her, smiling, a gift clutched in both hands, wrapped in Thomas paper — blue with little engines all over it, a shiny bow on top.

"I love it," Harry said. "It's so wonderful, I don't want to cut it. That'll ruin it."

"I've taken a picture, so you'll have the memory. Cakes are for eating," she said. "And it's a double celebration."

"What do you mean?" He frowned.

"Open this." Milton thrust the present at Harry. To prevent Cook from saying more?

Uncomfortable and out of sorts, Harry thanked him and took it, peeling back the wrapper carefully — he'd keep the paper forever. And there, in a white box, was a large knife, the last one he needed to complete his chef's set. Cook and Milton had been buying them for him each birthday for years.

"Oh, that's gorgeous." He stroked the box. "My Gorgeous."

"A beauty, isn't it?" Milton asked. "That's you on your way to coping on your own."

"Yes, and it's handy you have them all now, because you won't be able to pinch mine," Cook said.

Milton jabbed her side with his elbow.

"Oi!" she said, rubbing it. "No need to be so rough."

"Let the lad enjoy his day, then tell him," Milton admonished.

"What's going on?" Harry sensed something major was happening.

"Nothing," Milton was quick to say.

"Everything," Cook blurted at the same time. "Sit down, Harry love."

He did, shaking, a sense of terrible foreboding streaking through his blood, leaving him cold and shivery. "Tell me."

Cook and Milton sat, and Cook lit the candles on the top tier.

"You need to blow the candles out first and make a wish," she said.

They sang the birthday song to him, and he pushed air out to douse the eighteen twinkling lights, plus the one for luck. He wished . . . he wished that Cook and Milton were his parents, not his beast of a dead father and a mother who was off out somewhere, no doubt tending to those refuge women instead of being with him on this special day. He wished he could run far away from here and set up home elsewhere, together with the cook and the gardener, happy and content.

"Okay, now you can spill the beans," he said.

Cook shuffled, clearly uncomfortable, eyes filling. "There's no easy way to tell you this, darlin', but we're leaving. All of us. Me, Milton, the other staff. We were given our walking papers this morning, along with a month's pay. Your mother doesn't want us here anymore."

Harry's world imploded, and he stared at the two people he loved most. It couldn't be true, could it? Not after what they'd vowed to him. "But you said . . . you said you'd never leave me. When I was little, you told me you'd always be here, no matter what."

"And we meant it," she said. "But you're a man today, and your mother . . . Seems she wants you to do all our jobs instead of us, and won't that be nice? You're getting a wage and everything."

"Why do I need a wage when I don't leave this house? I'm too bloody scared to, she saw to that." He gritted his teeth to stop himself from crying.

They'd promised. They'd said he'd never be alone with her except in the evenings when they went home.

But they'd lied.

He stormed out, vision blurry, and ran to The Study, to think, to contemplate a life with just him and Mother in it.

He couldn't imagine it at all.

* * *

His first foray outside into the real world came with Mother taking him to the refuge. Oh, he'd driven the motorbike and her car around on the grounds, Milton teaching him how, but it wasn't the same as the jaunt on the open road. Everything was so frightening, so noisy and crowding, the buildings seeming to suddenly sprout out of the ground and loom over the car as they passed. In the city centre, shouts drifted through the open windows, so many people, all of it overwhelming. He cowered against the car door, eyes shut, heart pounding, mouth dry.

"Whatever's the matter?" Mother asked.

He sensed them turning a corner and cracked his eyes open. They travelled on an empty road now, and he calmed a little. "It's terrifying."

"Well, you'll only ever have to get used to this trip. That's the only place I'll take you, and remember, you can't run, even at the refuge. There are iron gates which are locked. You can't get out unless I'm there."

He imagined she'd told the staff he mustn't leave without her, and at home, he couldn't get out—the windows had had locks for as far back as he could remember, and the doors were secured from the outside if she went off anywhere, leaving him trapped indoors. And that had been okay all his life, because he hadn't had the courage to break free. Except now, since Cook, Milton, and the other staff had gone, he had the urge to search for them in this crazy, big city, to branch out and find himself, become a new person.

Spread those clipped wings of his.

Still, though, her threat of someone being out there, waiting to kill him, and Mother herself promising to do the same . . . well, perhaps he'd remain inside after all, too afraid to disobey her. Eighteen years of conditioning. Eighteen years of only knowing things a certain way.

Could he defy her and insist he had a life of his own?

Many years later, he did that, after spending time at the refuge and learning how to interact with other people, discovering TV, learning of the internet, sitting in on the therapy sessions that taught the women how to move past what they'd been through.

He'd used it as a tool to help himself. He'd gained courage, and although the row in the drawing room that had come before him storming out, getting in her car, and driving into the city for the first time alone was fraught with apprehension and a panic attack, he'd managed it.

People could overcome anything, given the chance and choice.

No one had come to kill him. Mother hadn't either.

Instead, he'd killed her.

CHAPTER SIXTEEN

The burger van owner, Quinn Upton, and his wife, Zoe, sat beside each other on a grey, crushed-velvet sofa. It was a nice, clean living room in one of the bigger houses on the Heights. A plug-in air freshener wafted the scent of vanilla, while a lit Yankee candle added to the aromatic ambience, although the couple appeared far from relaxed, and who could blame them, having the police here at such an hour?

Mike stood in front of the doorway.

Bethany, to his left, forced herself to get through this. Lethargy had a mind to push her towards one of the armchairs, but if she sat, she might never get up again. "Like I said when we arrived, so sorry to disturb you late in the evening, but we have a few questions regarding the area around your static van, and unfortunately, it can't wait until the morning."

Quinn sighed, seeming to expect a load of hassle, like he'd been through similar before. "If there's any rubbish, that's nothing to do with us." He scratched his head, short brown hair rasping from where gel or wax set it in hard spikes. "We clear the site every evening after we leave. It's part of the agreement with the council. We even take the black bag from the bin with us — and that isn't down to us, but it gets too full and isn't good for business, napkins and whatnot spilling out. Some people have been fly-tipping there, and we have to ring the council for them to collect it. Drives us nuts. Once, we had a sofa plonked right in front of the van. Scabby old thing, it was."

"It's not about rubbish." Bethany smiled sadly. "I only wish it was."

"What *is* it about then?" Zoe's huge green eyes were too big for her pale, elfin face. Her blonde pixie cut suited her, but she could do with eating a few of the burgers they sold. Skinny.

Bethany contemplated the options. Sidle around the subject or just tell them the truth? The truth won — these people wouldn't be going to work tomorrow or even the next day, not until the scene was released, so she needed to be upfront, prevent them from turning up there and contaminating the area.

She cleared her throat. "I'm just going to be blunt and get it out there, okay? I'm afraid someone might have been buried in the field behind your van."

"You *what*?" Quinn shot to his feet, grabbing his head either side, eyes darting about, his breathing erratic.

Panic, but whether from culpability or plain old innocent fright, Bethany wasn't sure yet. Whatever it was, he appeared unstable for a moment, someone to be wary of.

Mike stiffened, uneasy with the display. "Please sit down, sir." Stern: *Do as you're told.*

Quinn obeyed and took Zoe's hand, squeezing. It could be for comfort — but also to tell her to remain silent and let him do the talking. Everyone was a suspect in this game, and reading body language was a must.

"Do you mean we've been working there while someone's *dead*?" Quinn asked, voice croaky, cheeks going red.

Zoe whimpered, and tears fell. She was genuinely distraught. "Oh my God . . ." She shivered, probably imagining a grave right at her back while she'd flipped burgers and dished up chips into polystyrene cones, sprinkling them with salt and vinegar, blissfully unaware.

Until now.

With that reaction, Bethany decided these two had nothing to do with it. They were just unfortunate business owners who'd been caught in this horrific web. Someone else's actions had a hand in shaping their life, their thoughts, and they'd never be the same again.

"When . . . ? How long?" Yes, Zoe definitely had to be thinking back, considering the possibility that a corpse had maybe been there for days, decomposing a stone's throw away.

"We won't know until the body has been unearthed." It was at least twenty-four hours if the letter and map had been posted yesterday, but who knew, the killer could have waited to send the mail, having buried the body days ago. "Did you notice anything out of place this morning? What time do you arrive there?"

Quinn shook his head. "We always set up at five, ready for six. There are a few lorry drivers who come past early, wanting a bacon roll or whatever. A cup of tea. And no, I didn't see anything out of place." He frowned, maybe searching his mind in case he'd forgotten something.

"I did. That road sign had been moved." Zoe turned to him, holding his forearm with both hands. "Remember? It was at the edge of the lay-by where they'd fixed that hole last month, and no one had bothered coming to collect it, even though I'd phoned and reported it. Then it was dumped beside the van."

"I didn't even notice that," her husband said.

"Was that today?" Bethany asked, her spirits lifting, then dashing, because there was no CCTV on that road, so spotting who had been there wasn't on the table.

Zoe nodded. "It was definitely there recently, in the lay-by, I mean, because I nearly reversed into it as we were leaving one night. I got arsey about the council not picking it up and rang them again when we got home, leaving a message that they didn't bother returning. But I can't recall which evening that was, just that I saw it by the van this morning, shoved in the grass."

The day had been so long it may as well have been two merged together, and Bethany had trouble keeping things straight in her head, so she understood how Zoe felt. If the body still hadn't been revealed when they got back to the scene, it might be an idea for her and Mike to jot down a timeline while they waited in the car. Or not. It depended on how tired they were. They could have a cheeky nap instead.

"Okay," she said. "Anything else?"

"I can't think," Quinn said. "This has knocked me for six. It's like my brain doesn't want to work."

"I can imagine." Bethany had sympathy for them. "I'm afraid you won't be able to open the van or move it to another location while a crime scene is ongoing. It'll be dusted for prints — technically, it's a piece of evidence until it's been given the all clear. We're treating it as murder."

"It's okay," Zoe said. "Us losing a few days of money compared to someone being killed . . . It doesn't matter at all."

"No." Quinn rubbed his face, stubble shushing. "I agree with you there. Fucking hell, that poor person and their family."

Bethany needed to push on. There was still so much to do once they left here. "What time do you shut up shop and leave?"

"We close the hatch at six, leaving by six-thirty after we've cleaned the grills and collected the rubbish," Quinn said. "We're not some greasy spoon."

Did I imply they were? She'd let that one go. He was uptight, and understandably so.

"Did you perhaps notice any vehicles coming by before today, maybe slowing as they passed you, or even parking up? Any customers who seemed off to you?" Bethany asked.

"There was that one man on the motorbike," Zoe said. "Do you know who I'm on about, Quinn? He talked dead posh."

Motorbike. Posh . . .

Mike raised his eyebrows then lowered his head to write notes.

"What, that bloke with the old-fashioned helmet, like he was out of the forties?" Quinn frowned. "Yeah, he's stopped by a couple of times in the last week. Not seen him before that."

"The time I remember him, he ordered a coffee and mentioned the road sign," Zoe said. "Said it wasn't just men at work, but a woman as well, meaning me. He laughed, thought it was well funny. I laughed, too, just because that's what you do with punters, but I didn't find it amusing at all. It was like . . . oh, I don't know. He was childish. And he left the coffee behind, ignoring me when I called out for him to get it."

"Now you've said about it, he was a knob, wasn't he." Quinn shook his head as if bringing the biker's face to mind.

Bethany grabbed the chance to ask, "What did he look like?"

"Oh, he had a massive grey beard. And I'm talking long," Zoe said. "The end reached halfway down his belly. And he had goggles on because his helmet didn't have a visor. Couldn't see his hair, obviously, but his eyebrows were brown, and that stuck in my head because of the beard being grey. Blue eyes. I'm sure about that because they were a cold blue, know the sort I mean?"

Bethany's heart sank. Harry had a neat, short beard — but he did have blue eyes. And what was with the goggles and an ancient helmet? The search Leona had done hadn't thrown up a driving licence or any vehicles belonging to Harry — only Margaret's car was down at that address. Vehicles in the past had shown a motorbike, belonging to Elias Allthrop, Harry's dad, but it had been registered as off the road in the eighties. Could Harry still have it? They'd need a warrant to search the premises, and that would take time, seeing as it was so late. *Shit.*

She whispered to Mike, asking him to set that in motion, and he left the room. They'd perhaps have it by the morning. Maybe not first thing, but before lunch. She hated to do this to Harry, seeing as he'd had such a terrible upbringing, but fingers were pointing firmly in his direction, and she couldn't ignore that, no matter how he'd been treated in the past.

"All right, I'll leave you be now." She handed over her card. "If you think of anything else, give me a call, and if I don't answer, send a text. You've been extremely helpful giving us a description; you have no idea how much I appreciate that. Again, sorry to have disturbed you." *In more ways than one.*

Quinn showed her out, and she joined Mike in the front garden, where he was still on the phone. It was too cold to hang about waiting for him, so she indicated she was going to the car and, once inside, closed her eyes for a moment. They stung with tiredness. Her whole body seemed full of lead, and her mind was sluggish, desperately trying to function for her but warning that it might conk out at any moment.

She cracked her eyes open and reached for the glove box, taking out a packet of scented wet wipes. Cleaning her face with the cold cloth revived her somewhat, but she could really do with a shot of espresso to shock her system back to life.

With Mike beside her, she drove off towards the city, the blanket of lights in various shades of white and a few amber or red, too many to count. She veered into a service station that was open late. It squatted on a turning off the roundabout, and Mike groaned.

"Just what I need." He pointed to a Costa sign. "I'm seriously running on fumes here."

"Me, too."

She parked, and they walked inside. Bethany was glad to be in the warm, although that might prove detrimental and lure her to sleep. Mike ordered and paid, and they took their coffees — an espresso and a latte each, it was *that* kind of day — and sank into the squidgy red booth chairs. Lethal; they could end up nodding off. Bethany went to watch the headlights of traffic going by but was greeted with her reflection and that of the tables and chairs instead.

"My feet are banging." Mike leaned back to get comfy. His face was pasty, folds showing how tired he was.

"Snap. I feel like I've been pulled through a hedge backwards. We'll get naff all sleep, then have to do this all over again tomorrow." She massaged her temples, and even that seemed like too much effort. "If you think about it, we've had shit loads of information thrown at us today inside, what, fourteen hours, that it's a wonder we're still functioning." She read the clock on the wall. "Okay, make that fifteen hours. It's eleven o'clock."

"Fucking hell." Mike sipped his espresso. "We're going to be jittery and wired after these."

"I don't care. I need it."

"If we hadn't driven past that burger van, we'd be tucked up in bed by now," he grumbled.

"I know, but I'm glad I went that way, aren't you? We'd have been scratching our heads as to the body location for days otherwise, like we were with Margaret."

"Hmm. It's seeming more and more likely Harry has something to do with this," he said.

"He must have a fake beard."

"Yep. So the intent was there all along. Right. Let's hash this out. Two locations close to his home — the van and Four Peaks. His mother's death. Let's say he paid Parker to dig the hole, Parker possibly got Cribbins to mess with the cameras at Wind Energy, then for whatever reason, Harry killed them — to keep them quiet or tie up loose ends. How would someone like him know people like them? Did he just walk into the Shank on the off chance, spotted a man who seemed like he'd be up for a bit of thieving, and approached him? I can't see Harry in a place like that by choice, to be honest, can you? Those three men don't run in the same circles." He finished his espresso. "To be fair, we don't know that much about Harry at all, do we. He hasn't got a footprint like most people, other than staying home for most of his life."

"He does have something," Bethany said. "I noticed, on the whiteboard, that Leona had done his financials. His name is on a credit card account along with Margaret's, but there were no anomalies. Two hundred pounds a week had been withdrawn for the past six months, plus it was used for petrol, shopping and the like. The balance was paid off in full each month from Margaret's bank account. He has one, and it contains the sum total of one hundred pounds a week going in, dating back to his eighteenth. No withdrawals, which is weird. Margaret's has a staggering amount of money in hers. Put it this way, Harry won't have to worry for the rest of his life, and he doesn't need to be frugal either."

"Providing it isn't him. If it is, he'll have plenty to give him anxiety once we've nabbed him."

"He just doesn't seem the type, though. I know I had an odd feeling about him, but he seems so innocent." She necked the remaining mouthful of espresso then started on her latte. Smooth. Bloody nice.

Mike laughed. "Does anyone seem the type?"

"I suppose not. They don't all go round with mad eyes like Peter Sutcliffe or Dahmer, do they."

Her phone beeped.

"Fuck, I bet that's Isabelle." She tugged her phone out.

It was.

Isabelle: BODY FOUND. SAME MESSY FACE, AMONGST OTHER THINGS. FEMALE.

Amongst other things?

Bethany: OKAY. ON OUR WAY.

"Bollocks. No rest for the wicked," she said. "How many SOCOs did Isabelle bring with her, did you notice?"

"Four, plus her."

"Okay, I can stretch to coffees for them and Glen, unless you want to go halves."

"Yep, fine by me."

They finished their drinks, used the loo, then ordered some flat whites for the others. She grabbed sugars and stirrer sticks, then drove them back to the scene. Stopping at the cordon, she passed Glen a coffee through the window. While Mike went off to distribute the to-go cups into waiting hands in the field, Bethany joined Glen on the roadside.

"Did many cars come this way while we were gone?" she asked him.

"Three after the first one. Thanks for this, by the way. It's turned bloody cold out here. This'll warm me up nicely."

"You're welcome. What about a motorbike?"

"No," he said.

Maybe Harry had decided to stay at home and watch his new TV. He might not be the type to want to return to the place where he'd dumped a body. *If it's him.* Some people were too afraid to come back.

She had to bear in mind that while suspicion was rife and alarms blared, coincidences were real, and sometimes, indications proved to be red herrings — or what she wanted them to mean.

Mike called to her, and, at the car, they put on their protective clothing again. She walked down the slope with him, slipping from the booties on the damp grass. A SOCO ferreted about along the way a bit, sipping his drink, and arcing his torch beam over the ground. The halogen bright inside the tent, they went in, the mound gone now, the mud from it placed in plastic containers to be sifted through and analysed at the lab. Two SOCOs worked the area surrounding it. The photographer had abandoned his picture-taking and, on his knees, examined a patch of long grass intently, camera dangling from his neck. Isabelle stood beside the body, staring down at it while cradling her coffee cup.

Bethany gave the body her attention, too. "Oh. I see what you meant in your text now."

"Oh, indeed. Slightly different this time." Isabelle drank, her breath coming out cloudy afterwards.

It *was* different. The woman had the filed-off face and missing eye, but she also had a gaping neck. The line wasn't straight, though — it went in a higher direction halfway along, a slanted line, then continued across to just below the ear. Perhaps the victim had moved or the killer had hesitated, panicked by the amount of blood that came out of a wound like that. That blood had either seeped into the mud beneath her or had made a big mess elsewhere. If elsewhere, someone had a big cleaning job on their hands.

Apart from the injuries, the woman appeared as though she'd just reclined for a nap. Her black sequin dress was obviously expensive, as were her cerise shoes and handbag, the latter resting on her belly, her hands placed over it as though, in life, she'd have done the same to prevent anyone from stealing it. Her skin was exceptionally white, like she was the type to purposely avoid the sun to get a vampire vibe.

She had either tights or stockings stuffed in her mouth. Beige.

"Jesus." Mike pressed a finger and thumb to his eyebrows. "The neck and whatever is in her mouth . . . specific for this person? Got to be, hasn't it?"

"I'd say so." Bethany nodded. "The others were all the same, apart from Margaret being naked, although Presley hasn't sent a message as to whether Parker and Cribbins are missing parts of their arses. We could go with the stockings just being handy to shut her up, signifying she screamed a lot. As for her neck slice, well, maybe it was a random act, off the cuff. She kicked up a fuss, and it was all they could do to subdue her, keep her quiet."

"Whatever, it's a nasty sight and a painful death — *if* she was alive at the time," Mike said.

"I'll soon tell you." Presley came in and walked towards them.

Everyone said hi to him, and he did a quick sketch of the body's position on his clipboard, then got to work laying out some plastic sheeting, kneeling on it. He leaned over the body, nodding and muttering to himself for a while. Isabelle sipped her coffee, and the photographer snapped another picture, the sound of the shutter seeming overly loud.

"There's something here, Izzy," the SOCO said.

Isabelle went over there. "Ooer. Lovely." She bent over to part the patch of long grass. "A porn DVD."

"Blimey," Mike said. "Could have been dumped. The owners of the burger van said people throw stuff here."

"Could be, but we'll bag it just the same." Isabelle returned to stand with them.

Presley straightened up. "Well, it's the same as the others with regards to the tool used to take out the eye. Also inserted into her ear with force — tasty. I finalised Margaret's PM this evening — thought I'd better put in some overtime, what with the body count rising — and cause of death is the screwdriver penetrating the brain. I suspect they'll all have died in the same way. Now this lady could have an identical cause of death, and I'm going to put it out there that her neck was sliced soon afterwards, not before. I say that because the bloodstains on her skin are fluid, coating it, not coagulated, which would happen fifteen minutes after death. It thickens then and would seep out in a different way. Think water versus honey. As you can see, that's not a honey-type drip."

"More a watery gush," Bethany agreed.

"Precisely." Presley squinted up at Isabelle. "Want me to open her bag while I'm down here?"

"If you change your gloves first. There's blood on them."

He obliged her then drew a phone out of her bag.

Isabelle took it. "Password protected. Not a problem for digi forensics, just annoying for us. What else is in there?" She popped the phone in an evidence bag and wrote details on it.

Bethany took some more from a nearby box so Presley could put whatever he found in them.

"Lipstick." In the bag. "A small mirror." In the bag. "And a purse."

"Open it then," Isabelle said.

He did, pulling out a driver's licence. "A Selondra Imes."

"Pardon?" Bethany's heart rate scattered. "Show me that." She held her gloved hand out and took it. Yep, Selondra Imes, her date of birth and address. UK flag to the right, her photo to the left. She was pretty, brunette. And she knew Harry Allthrop. "This has cemented it for me. We're after Allthrop. Mike, can you ring up and ask for that warrant to be fast-tracked, please."

He exited the tent.

"This woman . . . I've been trying to get hold of her. Now I know why she hasn't been answering her phone." Bethany took in a deep breath. "She bloody couldn't."

"What's she got to do with Allthrop?" Isabelle asked.

"According to Diana at the refuge, Selondra was seeing Harry, but it didn't go anywhere on the grounds that he was 'shit in bed'."

"Oh. Nice."

"Presley, can you quickly peek at Selondra's backside for me?" Bethany asked.

He rolled the body onto its side and pulled up the dress. She had no underwear on, and her bum had been sliced.

"Oh God . . ." Bethany felt sick. "I'd better go. I need to see if she's been reported as missing, plus find out her next of kin. Will we ever get to bed tonight?"

"You might, but I doubt I will anytime soon." Isabelle pulled a sad face.

Presley got up. "I'm estimating, broadly. Time of death, a couple of days. Might be less. Like with Margaret, the soil plays a part. It's cold out, she was packed beneath it, so it messes with the body temperature. There's no bloat, so less than five days, but like I explained before, bloat can be held off until after that due to burial. Let the night staff know when she can be taken in, Isabelle. I'm going home."

"Lucky bastard." Isabelle poked her tongue out.

"Sorry." He shrugged and walked off.

"That's that then," Bethany said. "I hope you manage to at least get a kip. I'm off to the station."

"Night," Isabelle said.

"Night, love."

CHAPTER SEVENTEEN

Harry wheeled the motorbike down the side of the remote cottage and hid it in the shadows round the back beside the bamboo canes set up like teepee frames, ready for the runner beans to climb up them come planting time. Milton had always loved growing those.

Nostalgia hurt.

Harry kept the helmet and goggles on, ready for a quick getaway, and approached the front garden, which was pristine, as it should be when it belonged to a man keen on landscaping. In the light of the lamp glowing beside the door, he studied the area. Hedges in the shape of animals dotted the grass, five of them in all. Topiary was something Harry had learnt to master once Milton had left, and he was proud of his dragon, cat, and horned fairy.

The flowerbeds had been cleared, the mud turned over recently, ready for the oncoming winter, reminding him of the graves he'd dug, and the lawn edges, cut with Milton's special tool, brought back more memories, especially with the grass having short, uniform blades.

The cottage, now that was lovely. It could be described as quaint, wonky in places from the years poking and prodding at it. Harry hadn't been here since that day he'd requested answers Milton hadn't been able — or prepared — to give. All he'd said was he was sorry they'd had to go, and that working for Margaret wasn't for the faint of heart, and her giving them their marching orders had been a godsend, despite them having to leave Harry to the mercy of his mother.

That wasn't good enough. Harry had needed them, forever, and they'd let him down.

Since his eighteenth, when they'd walked out, Cook looking back at him over her shoulder, tears in her eyes, hate had festered. He'd gone on to plan everything to the tiniest detail. Although he hadn't banked on having to kill Aiden and John, it had worked out well enough. He'd let his idea ferment for many years, until one day, he'd known it was time.

He slid the stolen key in the lock and twisted it, stepping inside. All was silent, not a creak or whine coming from the hinges. There he was, in Milton's hallway, the stairs to the left, waiting for him to climb them. Leaving the door ajar, he ascended, taking his holdall off his back, opening it, and moving to the bedroom he knew to be Milton's — he'd fully inspected the place last time instead of using the bathroom like he'd said.

Door open, he focused on the figures in the bed, elderly now, lying on their sides, facing away from each other, a fair old gap between them.

Milton and Pam, still together.

He hated their closeness. Their love. A life that didn't include him.

He crept in, standing on Pam's side of the bed, and knelt, whispering close to her ear, "I'm about to break the lawah." A giggle popped out, and he clamped his lips together. He took a slim torch from his pocket and switched it on the low beam, positioning it on the nightstand so it pointed directly at Pam's wrinkled face. Her head. Grey hair. White nightie. Ruffles at the neck, buttons down the middle.

Milton stirred. Rolled onto his back. Groaned.

Harry waited. Waited. Decided it was time to move things along.

Holdall on the floor, he reached inside, bringing out My Gorgeous.

She stabbed herself into Pam's neck and stood up all by herself, nice and straight, proud of what she'd done. Pam jolted, and he tugged My Gorgeous out. The arcs of red fluid spurted in time with the beats of Pam's heart. He leaned close, closer, so he could see her eyes, open now, wide, but not as wide as her toothless mouth. What did he appear like to her with the helmet and goggles on? What did she see, think, feel?

She inhaled a long breath, ready to scream, but no sound came. Too much blood loss, and that blood, it gurgled in her throat, dribbled from between her lips, seeping down, spilling onto the pink flowery bedding. She choked, brought her hand up to the wound, and he could have told her it was useless but instead let her think she could stop the flow, could still live.

The light died in her eyes then, life gone, soul wending upwards, unseen but there, wishing it could cling to the body it had inhabited, only to find that body could no longer house it.

No room at the inn, Pammy.

Harry peered over at Milton. He had earplugs in and let out a rumble of a snore.

Harry got up and took his holdall and My Gorgeous to the other side of the bed, casting his gaze over the nightstand. A half-full glass of water sat on it, a packet of tablets, perhaps sleeping pills, perhaps not, but Harry thought that was what they were. Why else would this man not rouse when his wife was being killed?

He took the grater out and rasped it — hard — over the gardener's cheek. Harder. Again, again, until the old man slapped at it and groaned, eyes cracking open, two slits, then wider, wider still — *Milton can see me now!* — and Harry grabbed the screwdriver and plunged it in, beside the iris, pulling it back out amidst Milton's hoarse screaming, the eyeball on the end, strings of something he didn't want to think about hanging off it. My Gorgeous would cut them off later, and the prize would be put in the jar. Like the eggs in the fridge, those bloody eggs.

She whispered, that knife of his, whispered to him to stab the bastard in the guts, because Milton hadn't had any while working for Mother — none to stand up to the wicked bitch, none to insist he'd take Harry away to a safer place. They all knew how she'd treated him, and they'd let it happen, too scared of her to do otherwise, needing the wages, times being hard.

They should have saved him.

Milton screamed, on and on, loud and harsh, and Harry couldn't bear it. He scrabbled in his bag for the arse jam, using a spoon to ram Selondra's flesh into the man's mouth, filling it to the brim, Milton heaving, choking.

"Eating is nothing but torment," Harry whispered.

Flashes of his childhood streaked through his mind — Milton wiggling his fingers in the garden, flapping his ears. Slipping Harry some sweets and bringing his finger to his mouth: *Shh, don't tell your mother!* Kicking a ball with him. Milton, Milton, fucking Milton . . .

My Gorgeous embedded herself in the man's heart.

A wheeze. A rasp of air. A grater-wrecked face. A bleeding eye socket.

He was gone after a while, dead, and My Gorgeous leapt out of the body, telling Harry he hadn't done a thing, that it was her, all her.

A naughty, grudge-filled knife.

Good girl.

* * *

"You have to stop going out alone," Mother said, pacing the kitchen.

"That doesn't wash with me anymore. I'm going into the city. There are things I need to buy. Selondra suggested them."

"They'll come and get you, take you away from me."

He wished whoever it was had done it years ago.

"Are you insane?" he asked. "I've often wondered that. No one will kill me. Whatever gave you that idea? You never did say."

She told him then, about his father, things no son should ever have to hear — beatings, rape, manipulation, and all the while, she'd let her little boy suffer, long after Father had died. She'd become a different person to the one he remembered from the early days, the one who'd cuddled him, kissed him, and told him before bed that one day, they'd leave. She'd pack a bag, and they'd run away together, just her and him.

Things had changed after that.

Mother continued her story, saying Father had heard her assuring Harry they'd be gone soon, and he'd put measures in place so they couldn't.

The threat that he'd have her precious son murdered.

"I was horrible to you to keep you safe," she said. "Don't you see?"

No, he didn't.

She rambled on, her words meaning nothing except to fix it in his head that she'd stopped loving him and had allowed a man to frighten her into believing what he'd said was true. And wasn't that ironic? She'd learnt from the master and employed the same tactics on Harry, ensuring he'd remained indoors or on the grounds for years, a lifetime, until the urge to find out what the world was like had pushed him to defy her and visit the city without her.

He grabbed the grater that hung on a wooden drying rack suspended from the ceiling, pots and pans clattering with the force of the snatch. "See this?" He advanced towards her, anger fuelling, burning.

"No!" she said, hands flying up to her face, because she knew, she fucking knew he intended to give her a taste of her own medicine.

And he did, shoving her to the floor and sitting on her, grating, grating her cheek, My Gorgeous cheering in the background, shouting, "Kill the bitch! KILL HER!"

Mother fought, writhed, but her agony was no match for his temper. He stripped her, grated her backside, blood, so much blood, her wails musical, a delight. Finally, he'd done to her what she'd done to him.

He was his mother's son. Like she'd turned into his father, Harry had turned into her, and so went the circle of abuse.

"I've got somewhere for you to go, and you can think about what you've done. Like The Study," he said, "only it's deeper, cold, filthy, and dark like your heart."

He tied her up, shoved a rag in her mouth, right to the back of her throat so she gagged. Bound her to the radiator pipe, the rope coarse on her wrists. Left her there until night came with its shrouding cloak. In the garage, he attached the ancient sidecar to the motorbike then stuffed her in it, driving to Shadwell Hill, to the hole that had been dug so recently, one he wasn't sure he'd have the courage to use, but here they were.

And it was a relief.

He tied her wrists, threw her down into the pit, and she was still naked, exposed, vulnerable.

Then he covered it over with branches and autumn's fallen leaves, knowing whatever sounds she made would be small, pitiful, and unheard.

* * *

He returned the next night, tossing energy bars and a drink down to her, mimicking what she'd done that time when he'd been locked in The Study for days. He'd also had a Thermos and those food bars, and he'd only nibbled every so often to make them last. There had been no telling when she'd come back to let him out.

He covered the piece of hole he'd created to give her the food and flask, put up the workman's sign and the rope cordon, then rode home, thinking she could rot in the hole, die all alone, just as she deserved.

He'd left a message with The Shadwell Herald, *telling them she'd gone to the Cotswolds.*

Three days she was in that forest, then he decided to get her out, kill her, and bury her. She gripped the rope, her lifeline, and he hauled her up. She cried, pitiful, self-indulgent, and anger arrived inside Harry once more.

"Don't you dare cry," he snapped.

His torch, propped behind a large stone on the ground, fully lit half of her form and faintly showcased the other. She held her hands up to her mouth, her filthy, mud-stained hands, where she'd probably tried to claw her way out. The wrist rope dug into her skin. Her body shook, and she turned her back to him, possibly through shame but more to show she still had the fire in her to do as she damn well pleased.

He was about to put that fire out.

Mud streaked her arse, and where he'd grated, it had become infected.

He was happy about that.

My Gorgeous called him from the holdall, and he obeyed her, picking her up and approaching Mother. He shoved her to the ground, and she landed face-first. He was on her legs inside a second, slicing off that wound, Mother screaming so hard that eventually no sound came out. He lobbed the arse into his bag and grabbed the screwdriver. Twisting Mother onto her back, he glowered down at her dirty face, wet with tears, her chest rising and falling fast.

"You promised to do that to me once, didn't you," he said. "Does it hurt? Does your backside sting?"

She whimpered, and he raised the screwdriver.

It found its way into her eye.

"Pickled egg," he breathed, euphoria winging through him as he pulled the eye out.

Mother wouldn't shut up. Wouldn't stop bucking. He flung the eye into the holdall. Stared at her pain-contorted face. And drove the screwdriver into her ear.

CHAPTER EIGHTEEN

"Selondra is down as missing," Bethany said, leaning on Mike's desk, the filed report on the screen.

"Shit." He stood by the coffee machine, stirring their drinks. "Who by?"

"Her sister, the next of kin. Parents died in twenty-twelve." She'd pulled up details on Selondra to find other relatives.

"Where does she live?"

"With Selondra."

"Oh . . . Shall we drink this then go there?" He spied the time. "Fuck's sake. Where did the last two hours go?"

"I don't know, but I want my bed more than I ever have."

She wheeled a spare chair over so Mike could sit beside her. She studied the screen again. Selondra owned a BMW, and Bethany wrote down the personalised reg number: SEL IIM. She Googled the cost of something like that, and similar came in at a price range of over five grand. Selondra had money, which wasn't surprising if she'd dated Harry Allthrop.

She closed the browser. There would be mail in her office, waiting for her to open it, but honestly, she was shattered. It would have to wait.

Mike plonked down, and they drank, Bethany's mind blank for a blissful moment. The Costa coffee hadn't done much except allow her to get through until now, but she dreaded to think how she'd have coped without it.

"How are we dealing with Harry once the warrant comes through?" Mike asked.

"We need to get a glimpse of that motorbike, see if it's in working order or if he's even still got it. That's just a guess on our part, maybe a massive hope. I suppose we'll play it by ear once we get there."

Her message alert jingled.

> Isabelle: I'VE SIGNED OFF THE ROAD AND LAY-BY, SO GLEN IS ON HIS WAY BACK. SELONDRA HAS BEEN TAKEN IN, AND THE SCENE WILL BE CHECKED AGAIN IN THE MORNING — THE WHOLE FIELD WILL BE SCOURED, BETTER IN DAYLIGHT. WE FOUND SOMETHING ODD IN HER SHOE — A PIECE OF WHAT LOOKS LIKE WRAPPING PAPER, ABOUT TWO INCHES SQUARE, WITH THOMAS THE TANK ENGINE ON IT. NO IDEA WHAT THAT'S ABOUT. I REMOVED THE STOCKINGS FROM HER MOUTH, AND WHAT APPEARS TO BE JAM WAS SITTING AT THE BACK. PUT THERE AFTER DEATH? ANYWAY, I'M OFF TO MY BED. SPEAK TOMORROW.

> Bethany: WHAT THE HELL? OKAY, SLEEP TIGHT.

She regarded Mike, her mind spinning slowly instead of at its usual frantic pace. She needed sleep to process this, but that wasn't going to happen.

Struggle on it is, then.

"More work?" Mike asked.

She told him what Isabelle had said.

"Eh? Jam? Thomas?" He frowned, rubbing his forehead. "And why didn't he slice off the men's backsides? What's that about?"

"No bloody idea. Margaret, Parker, and Cribbins didn't have the jam or the Thomas paper. Maybe random things come to him when he's killing, and he just goes with it." She sipped until her cup was half full, then stood. "I don't know about you, but I want to get this over and done with. Selondra's sister, I mean." She found her name on the monitor. "Victoria Imes." Stretching her arms up eased out some of the muscle ache. "Come on. I need a wee first, though."

* * *

Outside, the crisp air slapped her, bringing on welcome alertness — or maybe that espresso had finally kicked in properly. Whatever, she was grateful for the second wind and drove them to the address, which turned out to be one of the new swanky apartments down by the river, ground floor, glass-fronted. She pressed the buzzer for number two and rubbed her arms, her body chilled from sleep deprivation as well as the weather.

It took a few seconds, but a ravaged voice crackled out of the speaker. "Selondra? Did you lose your key?"

"DI Bethany Smith and DS Mike Wilkins."

"Oh God . . . Oh no . . ."

A buzz, then the door lock released. Bethany and Mike walked into a marble-floored lobby, heading straight for the door with a fancy metal number two on it. A woman much like Selondra's driving licence picture opened up, eyes wide, shadows beneath, worry crimping her delicate features.

"Victoria Imes?" Bethany asked, holding up her ID.

"Yes, yes, come in. Have you found her?"

"Let's get inside, shall we?" Bethany moved past her and entered a living room, spacious and furnished by someone with expensive taste — white everywhere with black accents: vases, ornaments, lamps, a rug.

With everyone seated, Bethany said, "Do you have anyone we can call to sit with you?"

Victoria whittled her fingers. "W-why?"

"Do you?" Bethany pushed.

"My neighbour at number one."

Bethany nodded at Mike, and he strode out.

"I'm sorry to inform you that your sister's body was found earlier."

"Body?" Victoria blinked. "But that means . . . No. No . . . Not my sister! Not her . . ."

Bethany waited it out while Victoria cried; she moved to sit beside her on the sofa and held the woman's hand, her own tears stinging. How difficult it was now to comfort someone riddled with grief when she knew exactly what it felt like, that first rip into your soul, that indescribable black hole that yawned, mourning waiting on the other side, mouth open, ready to chew you up then spit you out into a completely different version of your world that was alien, confusing, and terrifying.

Mike returned with a young lady in her pyjamas, blonde hair sleep-tossed, eyes puffy and darting from Bethany to Victoria then back again.

"Oh, Vic . . ." She rushed to her friend's other side — Mike had obviously told her.

"We'll make a drink," Bethany said and let them be, finding the kitchen.

With Mike in there with her, she closed the door, grateful to find one of those hideously expensive taps that released boiling water. She collected two mugs from a cupboard and raised her eyebrows at Mike: *D'you want one?*

"No, thanks," he said. "Blimey, this is tough."

"It always is." She found the makings for tea and got to work. "I'm just going to ask the questions outright when we go back in. She needs some time to get to grips with this, so the sooner we can leave, the better." Bethany had wanted to be left alone, to crawl into a shell made of Hell and hate and bewilderment, and she imagined Victoria might want the same. She picked up the teas.

Mike opened the door, and they entered the living room. Victoria appeared more composed, clutching her friend's hand, face blotchy, eyelashes damp and clumped together.

"Here you go." Bethany handed them the mugs and sat beside Victoria. "Now, we need to find whoever did this, so I'm going to quickly ask you some questions, then we can get back out there and find them, okay?"

Victoria nodded.

"Do you know where Selondra was going when you last saw her?"

"Out for dinner, but she didn't say where."

"How did she get there?"

"She took her car."

There were no keys in her bag . . . "What was she wearing?"

"A black dress that has sequins on it. Pink shoes and a clutch."

"When did you realise she was missing?"

"The next morning. I went into her room to wake her up — she was supposed to do her shift at the refuge — but her bed hadn't been slept in. I rang her on and off all day, then, once it got to about eight o'clock, I called the police. They said to wait another twenty-four hours. I rang the refuge, and she hadn't turned up. I would have rung Mrs Allthrop, but with her being dead . . . Oh . . ." Tears came again, and she wiped them away with her fingers.

"You did everything you could," Bethany said. "Please don't blame yourself."

Victoria nodded. "What happened to her? You said you found her body, but . . ."

"She was murdered, love."

"How?"

You really don't want to know. "I don't think you're ready for the details yet."

"It's the same as Mrs Allthrop, isn't it?" Her bottom lip wobbled. "Oh God, no. Please don't say it is."

Her eyes were so saucer-like, giving her a trusting air, and Bethany wanted more than anything to tell this woman she hadn't guessed right, but her face must have said it all. Victoria wailed, and Bethany took the tea from her and placed it on the little table in front of them.

"I'm so sorry," she said. *You have no idea how much.* "We'll find whoever did this, all right?"

"It won't bring her back."

"No, it won't." What else could she say?

They stayed for another few minutes until Bethany was sure Victoria's friend could cope with her.

"Would you like the family liaison officer to visit you? She'll come right away if you need her." Bethany dreaded calling Alice to haul her out of bed.

That said, Alice wouldn't mind. She was devoted to the people who needed her.

"What good will that do?" Victoria asked.

"She'll talk you through everything, so you know exactly what will happen next. You can just chat to her, about anything you want, and she'll be there for you."

Victoria nodded.

"I'll ring her once we've left. Her name is Alice Jacobs, okay?"

Another nod.

With condolences offered and Bethany's card on the table, they walked away from a grief-stricken sister who clung to her friend as though if she didn't, she'd drown.

Bethany knew that feeling.

Too well.

* * *

The warrant came through just as they got in the car, Mike taking the call then ringing Ursula to arrange for two uniforms to join them at The Grange in twenty minutes. Bethany contacted Alice and asked her to get to Victoria's as soon as possible, reciting the address and giving her a brief synopsis of what had happened.

She drove to pick the warrant up, then they headed for Harry's place. A police car had parked on the roadside just before the turning to The Grange, and she butted up behind it, getting out to chat to the officers.

The driver's side window eased down, and she leaned on the lip of the door and peered in.

"Ah, Glen. Didn't expect to see you again so soon."

"Same here," he said, smiling.

Tory Yates sat in the passenger seat. "Morning, boss."

"Morning, although it doesn't feel like it. Still seems like yesterday to me. We haven't stopped." Calling it morning when it was the middle of the night and dark seemed weird. "Right, we have a warrant to search the premises. We're specifically wanting to find a motorbike, an old-fashioned helmet, some goggles, and a long grey beard. Anything else is just gravy."

"We'll follow your lead then," Glen said.

"Yep, tail me up the drive, and we'll go from there."

She returned to the car and led the way, headlight beams cutting into the darkness, and the house loomed out of night-time's veil, housing a possible killer who could act innocent when in reality he was a monster. Parked up, she rushed to the front door, waiting for Mike, Glen, and Tory to reach the step.

"Go round the back and left-hand side," she whispered to the uniforms. "Stand by the exits." She'd already noted there wasn't one to the right.

They nodded and disappeared. Bethany rang the bell, so awake now, the excitement of this being over soon lending her energy. Several seconds passed, then a light came on inside, shining through the glass in the door, and a Harry-shaped figure approached. He opened up in striped pyjamas, blinking sleep away.

Mike whistled to alert Glen and Tory, a message for them to come back. Harry winced at that, the piercing sound giving him a jolt.

"We have a warrant to search the premises," Bethany said, foregoing the hello, how are you?

Mike held it up.

"Excuse me?" Harry stared from the warrant to each of them in turn, incomprehension plastered on his face, then it smoothed out, and a flicker of fear or nervousness ticked beside his eye. "Gosh, do you think the killer planted something here?"

Oh, he was good.

"Please step aside, sir," she said, all formal, no nonsense.

Glen brushed past him, entering the house and vanishing into its depths.

"Garage key, sir?" Tory asked, gloved hand out.

"Oh, well . . ." Harry took the key out of the inside of the door and passed her the bunch. "This is most upsetting."

"Inside, sir." Mike stepped in and took Harry's elbow.

Bethany put gloves on and went with Tory to the garage. They pulled the door up together, and Bethany found a light switch, flicking it to bring the space into brightness. A black BMW sat to the left, SEL IIM on the plate, and right there was the gravy, the veg, the whole fucking roast dinner. A motorbike was tucked up front, a helmet and goggles dangling from the handlebars, a mop of hair that she assumed was the beard sitting on the seat along with a pair of pink knickers.

"It's him," she said. "Keep rooting — screwdrivers, a file rasp, a knife, anything."

She left Tory to it and steamed into the house, following the sound of voices to the living room. Harry ranted at this being a gross case of police misconduct, while Mike stood there listening.

Bethany took her cuffs off her trouser belt loop, keeping them at her back. She approached Harry and walked behind him, and as she slapped the cuffs on one wrist, she said, "Harry Allthrop, I'm arresting you on suspicion of four counts of murder. You do not have to say anything, but it may harm your defence if you do not mention when questioned something which you later rely on in court. Anything you do say may be given in evidence." She secured the other wrist.

"What?" he said, twisting to face her. "What the devil is going on?"

The devil is you. "We have found a car belonging to Selondra Imes, whose body was discovered earlier. A motorbike, helmet, goggles, beard, and women's underwear are also present on your property — the description of all the former was given to us by a witness. We will now search the rest of your house." *And we'll get a cast of that fucking kickstand and score a match for the divots.*

Mike shook his head, taking over by leading a clamped-lipped Harry from the room. She followed them, stopping at the front door, and watched Mike put him in the police car.

"Boss?" Glen called.

She went to find him. He was in the kitchen, his face pale with a green tinge. He pointed to the worktop.

"Oh, fuck me . . ." she said. "Um, bloody hell . . . Go and relieve Mike at your car. Ring Ursula and ask for more uniforms — we need help. This is a ruddy big house, and I don't want to be here all night. Tell Mike to come in here, please. Ask him to bring suits and booties."

Glen scooted out, gladly, she reckoned, and she'd do the same if she could.

She studied the items that had been placed in a row and shuddered. Harry was sick. He needed help. Bile rose into her throat, and she swallowed it.

Mike walked in, clothing in hand, then stopped short beside her. "Oh, fuck me."

"That's exactly what I just said." She'd laugh if things weren't so dire.

A grater, large knife, and a screwdriver sat beside a jar of eyes in what appeared to be malt vinegar.

Five eyes, not four.

"What the hell was going through his mind?" Mike asked.

"I have no idea, but I *can* tell you I'm glad there's not blood and gore on those weapons."

"So he used a cheese grater, not a file," he said. "Why? What even enters your head to think about doing that?"

"I don't want to contemplate it." She took booties from him and put them on. "There are five eyes. There's another body out there."

"Shit. Maybe we'll get another letter and map later."

"I hope so."

They got into the white suits, pulled the hoods up, and Mike slipped booties and gloves on.

"Isabelle is not going to be pleased," she said. "I bet the poor cow has only just got to sleep."

"No, she isn't too happy. I rang her while I was outside. I called for the meat wagon — I want that bastard taken in properly, locked up in it like he deserves."

"Cheers. I suppose we should get nosing about."

She walked around, poking in cupboards, then the fridge. "Oh. Shitting Nora. Come and have a gander at this."

Mike appeared beside her. "Jam."

"Yes, in a bowl, but see what's on that plate?"

He leaned forward then reared back. "What *is* that?"

"Looks like an arse cheek to me, with bits of flesh taken out. And in that other bowl, little balls of . . . well, seems like kitten biscuits, that kibble stuff. If you think about it, similar shapes are in the jam."

"Do we even want to think about what it is?"

"I don't, but it was put in Selondra's mouth." She closed the fridge and wandered through a door into a utility room. After inspecting the washing machine and tumble dryer and finding them empty, she strode into the kitchen and opened the dishwasher, zooming in on the filter in the base. "Ugh, that's suspiciously like flesh in there, except it's soggy and bloated where it's been in the water."

"Pack it in," he said. "I'm on the verge of being sick here."

She chuckled. "The joys of our job, eh?"

Then she spotted a Thomas the Tank Engine mug in the sink. Zoe Upton had called Harry childish, and this went some way to explaining that — plus the piece of paper left at Selondra's scene. Were they dealing with someone who hadn't grown up? He'd seemed adult enough to Bethany, but perhaps there was a kid locked inside him somewhere, one that came out every so often.

Several officers bustled in then, and the search got properly underway. Isabelle turned up with five SOCOs, and while The Grange became a hive of activity, Bethany and Mike lending a hand, minutes and hours slipped by. The next time she spied a clock, it was coming up to four a.m., and with no chance of sleep coming their way, she accepted the fact they'd be working until later today and might not get into bed until long after Harry had been questioned.

The find of the hour was blood in the dining room, which had been cleaned, but the forensic light had picked it up. Loads of it. Enough for a murder scene. A slit neck.

Macabre.

CHAPTER NINETEEN

Harry shivered in the cell they'd put him in, unable to comprehend what had happened. How had it all gone so wrong? And who was the witness who'd seen him in the beard? He couldn't recall speaking to anyone while it had been stuck to his face, but then, everything was a blur now, scenes and remembrances merging, past and present, creating a montage of mismatched sequences that didn't make sense and hurt his head.

The officers who'd brought him here had been abrupt, booking him in without sentiment, leaving him confused and out of sorts. His emotions were all over the place — he didn't feel anything like he thought he would when he'd imagined this happening. He'd thought he'd be strong, able to convince them he hadn't done anything wrong, yet here he was, cowering against the cell wall, the floor hard on his backside.

They'd found Selondra's car. Why hadn't he hurried up and dumped it? Why had he left it in the garage? Because he'd reckoned that driving it openly would bring attention to him. The plates were distinctive, and if Selondra's sister had reported her missing, the police would have been told to sight that vehicle.

Were they going through his house now, searching for things to prove he'd been a bit of a 'vile man'? They'd see My Gorgeous, the jar of eyes, and take them away from him. He'd left Thomas in the washing-up bowl, and they'd find him, too. How would his things cope without him?

He cried, for the boy he'd been and the man he was, but it didn't ease his mind or soul. He was as trapped by circumstances as he'd always been, and his plan had been stopped before completion. Cook still lived, and he hated those detectives for ruining things.

Hate. It festered in you. Always there. Burning.

* * *

On his fifteenth birthday, one of the presents Cook and Milton had clubbed together to buy him was a train set, complete with a Thomas engine and a Fat Controller. Cook had once told him about her weekend trip on the train to Edinburgh, where she'd had a lot of fun and memories to bring out whenever she felt like it, and he'd bugged her about that journey for years. He'd imagined the trees whizzing past, the fields, the villages, towns, and cities, the clouds hovering with their white bellies, which had turned greyer the closer she'd got to Scotland.

To stave off the stark reality of his world, he often thought of her tale, pretending he'd sat on the train with her. He'd handed the man their tickets. He'd gone off to the buffet car and brought them sandwiches and sweets, steaming tea in white polystyrene cups. He'd alighted at the station, helping her off, taking her tartan suitcase on wheels and pulling it behind them as they'd gone out onto the street to wait for the taxi to the bed and breakfast.

A year or so after he'd received the presents, he created his own world, talking to his toys as if they were real, unable to admit they weren't. He pushed Thomas along the track, the Fat Controller wicked, like Mother, bullying Thomas and setting him up for a fall time and time again.

Not long after that, he'd grated the Fat Controller's face off.

* * *

The police, they'd find his gifts. They'd see what he'd done to the plastic man in his black suit and top hat. They'd . . . they'd know he was as mad as Mother.

Throughout his teenage years and on into adulthood, he'd spoken to everything that belonged to him — My Gorgeous, those eyes, the bloody horrible eyes. He had nothing now. Nothing familiar. Nothing for comfort.

He looked down at his body, hunched as it was, and decided he had no alternative but to talk to himself. He was all he had left.

CHAPTER TWENTY

Fran and Leona had been briefed on the latest, and Bethany studied the whiteboard, checking to see if the information had been there all along but none of them had seen it. As far as she could tell in her overtired state at nine a.m. on a cold, foggy morning, sleep still a distant possibility, they'd cottoned on to it definitely being Harry after Selondra had been found, so they couldn't blame themselves for not apprehending him earlier.

She'd been in to see Kribbs, giving him all the details, and he'd ordered her and Mike to go home and get some shut-eye before questioning Harry. He could wait in the cells for a while, seeing as they had evidence stacked up against him and time wasn't of the essence. She hadn't argued — she was too bloody tired to — and now she turned to her team.

"Okay, me and Mike are going to shoot off for some kip. We'll be back by about four, then we'll discuss anything you've found while we're gone."

She pulled up outside Mike's, and he rushed in to grab some things. He came out with a large suitcase, and she grinned to herself while he put it in the boot. Him moving in was happening, and she felt nothing but happiness. She hoped Vinny would be cheering over this, and it gave her a sense of doing the right thing — for her and for Mike.

At her place, she crashed until the alarm woke her at three-fifteen, and she sat up in bed, actually feeling worse for the rest, and my God, she could just fall back onto the mattress and sleep for England. She had a work hangover, too many hours spent awake and not enough in the Land of Nod. Aching, limbs heavy, she forced herself into the shower, which did nothing much to revive her, then sat with Mike at the kitchen table, drinking coffee and munching on thick-cut toast as if it were seven in the morning, not quarter to four in the bloody afternoon.

Their body clocks were going to be well off for the next couple of days.

They arrived back at the station, and no sooner had they stepped into the incident room than her mobile rang. Rob's name was on the screen, and she sighed, really not wanting any more shit landing on her plate. She had paperwork to do, a killer to interview, and anything else . . . honestly, it could just go and do one.

"Hi," she said, aiming for bright but sounding narked.

"Sorry, boss, but there's two more bodies."

"Jesus Christ!" *Two? But there was only one extra eye in that jar.*

"A woman has been stabbed in the neck, a single wound. The other, a male, has the face issue, no eye, and was stabbed in the chest."

Okay. Right. That wasn't good.

"Where and who?"

"Rosewood Cottage, out in the sticks on Hallswift Road, owned by a Mr and Mrs Milton."

Why did that name ring a bell? She rushed to the whiteboard and scanned the information. "Okay, I know who that is. The man anyway. We'll go there now. Thanks." She shoved her phone in her pocket. "Guys, it looks like the Allthrop's old gardener has copped it, plus a woman."

Mike slapped his pen down on the desk. "For fuck's—"

"I know, I know. But we have to go." She smiled at Fran then Leona. "Wellness check on Noreen Withers, the cook, please. We need to know if she's alive."

The journey to Rosewood Cottage took fifteen minutes, but it felt as long as an hour. On the way, they'd chatted about what Mike would do with his furniture and had agreed that he needed some of his things around him, otherwise it'd feel like her place wasn't his home. It was good to discuss something other than the case, and by the time they arrived outside the cutest cottage she'd ever seen, they had a moving plan in place. He'd be installed by the weekend and start paying half the bills come the first of the following month. He'd rent his own place out to someone else.

It was unpleasant having to switch from nice, happy things to the ghoulish, but switch she did, signing the log that Nicola Eccles held out at the front door, then donning protective clothing. Inside, the place had a sombre air, SOCO dusting for prints and opening drawers, and Bethany and Mike were directed upstairs to a bedroom.

Isabelle, eyes red-rimmed and showing signs of serious fatigue, stood by the bed, peering over at an old lady. She straightened and lowered her mask. "Let's hope these two are the last of them, eh?"

Bethany nodded. The sight was revolting. Blood coated the quilt, bottom sheet, and pillows, some large patches, spatter in other places. The woman was on her side, eyes wide, her face carrying an expression of utter terror and shock. Had she stared into the eyes of her killer? A single, knife-blade-depth slit marred her neck, her hand up near it where she may have tried to stop the flow of blood.

Beside her, an old man was on his back, face grated — it seemed sicker now she knew what had been used to create the damage — eye missing, and a stab wound to his bare chest, grey, curly hairs dyed crimson. He had earplugs in, and Bethany's mind zipped back to the last big case in the summer, where they'd been used on the victims to keep insects trapped. In this instance, they were more than likely chosen to block out the rumble of snoring.

"He's the old gardener at The Grange," Bethany said absently. "I don't know who she is or if she has anything to do with that place."

"Pam Milton," Isabelle said. "I rang in for an identity on the pair of them. They married after both getting divorces from their previous spouses. She doesn't have children, he does, but the kids live in Jersey, so that's let you off the hook having to turn up and deliver the bad news."

Bethany felt wicked, but she was relieved. She couldn't take much more trauma, not until she'd slept for a good ten hours or more.

Presley walked in, and after he'd sketched the body positions then surveyed the bodies, he went on to say they'd been murdered during the night. "Um, there's jam in his mouth."

Bethany's stomach churned. "Ah, about that . . ." She told them of her suspicions — the slice of flesh in the fridge, the nodules in that bowl.

"Oh, fucking hell." Isabelle heaved. "I'll get on to the lab about it, ask them to fast-track processing the jam in Selondra's throat." She paused. Swallowed. "What if it's got arse in it, though?"

"Don't . . ." Mike held up a hand to stop her. "What a warped bastard."

"I hope you're talking about Harry and not me," Isabelle said.

A message alert halted *that* particular conversation, and Bethany read her screen.

Fran: NOREEN WITHERS IS FINE.

Bethany: TFFT! THANKS.

If Bethany enjoyed crime scenes like this, she'd stay here just so she didn't have to deal with interviewing Harry, but time was moving fast, and they needed to get on with things. They arrived at the station twenty-five minutes later — all right, she'd driven slower to put off the inevitable — and with one of the duty solicitors waiting for them, Rob collected Harry from the holding cell and marched him past Bethany and Mike, through into the corridor where the interview rooms were located.

Rob came back and dipped behind the front desk. "The solicitor wants ten minutes. He's read the charges so knows what's going on."

"Okay." She walked over to the vending machine and got the three of them coffees. Placing Rob's on the desk, she then sat with Mike in the empty civilian waiting area. No point going up to the incident room, plus, they deserved to take a breather. "We just need to get through this, then we can leave everything else until tomorrow."

Mike nodded, accepting the coffee. "Thanks. I don't have to tell you I'm glad you're leading on this. I don't think I'll be able to keep my feelings out of it. Who the fuck," he said, lowering his voice, "puts flesh in jam and feeds it to people, assuming that's what he's done? Does he think he's Hannibal Lecter or what?" He paused, musing. "There was this bloke, Vladimir Nikolayev, who passed off his victims' flesh as high-end cuts of meat — Allthrop is on the same level as him, the weirdo."

"The things you watch," she said. "Or was that from a book?"

"A documentary."

"Nice. I don't know how you can watch that shit when we deal with it at work."

He shrugged. "It's interesting."

The desk phone rang, and Rob picked it up. "Okay, I'll send them through." He replaced the receiver. "They're ready for you. Wait a sec while I rustle up a uniform to attend."

Bethany and Mike stood, drinking half their coffee then dumping the cups in the bin. Bethany sent a message to Fran, telling them to go home. They'd have a meeting in the morning to discuss any findings.

The uniform poked his head around the door leading to the corridor, and they all walked to interview room one. With everyone inside, the uniform positioned against the wall beside the exit, Bethany set up the recording equipment and ensured the video was on.

She said the official wording for the tape and, having decided earlier not to rely on a file full of crime scene photos of dead people to thrust under his nose, she dived in.

"Harold Clement Allthrop, you have been arrested on suspicion of the murders of the following people: Margaret Audrey Allthrop, Aiden Parker, John Cribbins, Selondra Imes, Stan Milton, and Pamela Emily Milton. What do you have to say to these charges?"

"They hurt me."

She held back a weary sigh. This old chestnut got old after hearing it as an excuse over and over again. "In what way?"

He shook his head. "It's too upsetting."

"Perhaps it is, but it's also upsetting that six people were killed because you were annoyed with them. If we all went round murdering people because we'd had our feelings hurt, there wouldn't be many people left on the planet, and we'd be in prison." *Where you're going, you bloody freak.*

The duty solicitor whispered in his ear.

Harry shivered. "I can't," he mumbled.

"It'll go in your favour, Mr Allthrop." The brief drummed his fingers on the table. He clearly didn't want to be here.

Neither do we, but ho pissing hum.

And Harry spewed the lot. Bethany reeled from the tale, the atrocities he'd suffered, the wicked awfulness of his life. She understood why he'd killed his mother but didn't condone it. He should have asked for help, but then again, with his sheltered upbringing, maybe he hadn't been aware that help was out there for him. In his warped reasoning, perhaps he thought aid only came for women at the refuge, not men like him.

He went on to tell her of his limited experience of the city, of life outside The Grange's walls, and her heart broke off piece by piece with each snippet he revealed. While she felt for him, she couldn't allow herself to fold completely — he'd killed people, and that she couldn't forgive him for.

His story took hours, with short breaks on the hour, and now, with the clock showing way after nine, she reckoned everyone in the room was wrung out and sickened by the words that had come out of Harry's mouth. She closed the interview, thinking about a little boy who'd had so much love from his mother for the first few years and then had it cruelly snatched away by a controlling father. A man who had manipulated his wife into behaving a certain way, sending her half crazy, and taught her to believe a killer was stalking her son long after her husband had died.

How had she kept the two halves of herself so separate? Diana at the refuge had said Margaret had some strange ways, and during their first encounter with Harry, he'd said his mother wasn't all there, or words to that effect. Margaret had appeared the consummate professional in front of the cameras, but the minute she'd gone home, she'd morphed into a bitter, spiteful woman who had wrecked her innocent son and turned him into a replica of herself to a certain degree — a man hell-bent on getting revenge for the way he'd been treated, while she'd raged over the ghost of a man she'd once married.

Bethany left the room with Mike, waving goodbye to Ursula, who had taken Rob's place behind the front desk, and plodded out of the station, knackered, head ringing from all that harrowing information.

At her place, she whacked a couple of microwave dinners in, poured herself a wine, and took a beer to Mike who'd flopped onto the sofa and gazed into space.

"I know I watch this sort of shit on the TV," he said, "But when I'm actually one of the players listening to what killers have to say, it seems a bit surreal."

"I know what you mean. Thank God it's over. I could sleep forever."

"Same." He cracked the beer can tab and took a long swallow. "Changing the subject . . . Are you sure about this? Me moving in, I mean."

"I wouldn't have asked if I wasn't. Just one rule, though."

"What's that?"

She took a sip of her wine, composing a straight face. "If you bring any ladies back, make sure to keep the noise level down in your bedroom, will you? The walls are thin."

He blushed and threw a cushion at her. "Piss off, you."

They laughed, far too hysterically, and she put that down to exhaustion. But it felt good to release some pressure after such a strange and tiring case.

The microwave dinged, pulling her back to reality, so she plonked her wine glass on the coffee table and shifted herself to dish up their food. Once she'd done that, she spotted her reflection in the window, blackness beyond. She caught her breath, swearing Vinny stood behind her, but when she spun round to face him, he wasn't there.

"Was that you?" she whispered, reaching out to touch the air, as if she'd feel him, solid beneath her fingertips. Had he shown himself to tell her he didn't want Mike living there? "Is that it — is that what you want?" she whispered again, thinking herself nuts. Ghosts didn't exist, only the idea of them did, but if it made her feel better, she'd believe they were real.

A soft whoosh of air brushed her cheek, and she raised her hand to capture it, keep it there, close, a part of Vinny. Then his laughter floated through her head, and she had her answer. Vinny didn't mind Mike being there at all.

And that lightened her steps as she carried their food into the living room, and they sat, side by side, eating macaroni cheese and staring at a blank TV, the smiling photo of Vinny beside it, once again giving her permission to move on and be happy.

I love you so much, Vin. Thank you.

THE END

THE JOFFE BOOKS STORY

We began in 2014 when Jasper agreed to publish his mum's much-rejected romance novel and it became a bestseller.

Since then we've grown into the largest independent publisher in the UK. We're extremely proud to publish some of the very best writers in the world, including Joy Ellis, Faith Martin, Caro Ramsay, Helen Forrester, Simon Brett and Robert Goddard. Everyone at Joffe Books loves reading and we never forget that it all begins with the magic of an author telling a story.

We are proud to publish talented first-time authors, as well as established writers whose books we love introducing to a new generation of readers.

We have been shortlisted for Independent Publisher of the Year at the British Book Awards three times, in 2020, 2021 and 2022, and for the Diversity and Inclusivity Award at the Independent Publishing Awards in 2022.

We built this company with your help, and we love to hear from you, so please email us about absolutely anything bookish at: feedback@joffebooks.com.

If you want to receive free books every Friday and hear about all our new releases, join our mailing list: www.joffebooks.com/contact

And when you tell your friends about us, just remember: it's pronounced Joffe as in coffee or toffee!

ALSO BY EMMY ELLIS

DI BETHANY SMITH

Book 1: THE COLD CALL KILLER
Book 2: THE CREEPY-CRAWLY KILLER
Book 3: THE SCREWDRIVER KILLER

DETECTIVE CAROL WREN MYSTERIES

Book 1: SPITE YOUR FACE
Book 2: HOLD YOUR BREATH
Book 3: GUILT BURNS HOLES
Book 4: BEST SERVED COLD
Book 5: BLOOD RUNS DEEP

Printed in Dunstable, United Kingdom

74319182R00109